Longarm fou[...] [...] [...]
way that migh[...] [...] [...]

He heard the sound of running footsteps in the back of the building, and followed them through a maze of trashed rooms.

"Stop or I'll shoot!" he yelled at the two men as they blasted out the back of the building into the alley.

Longarm went after them. When he exited the old ruined building into the alley, he saw that the two men had run headlong into a trap they could not escape because of a mountain of rubble from a fallen-in brick wall.

"You're under arrest!" Longarm yelled, raising his gun.

The two men dove in behind a mound of bricks, and a moment later they opened fire.

DON'T MISS THESE
ALL-ACTION WESTERN SERIES
FROM THE BERKLEY PUBLISHING GROUP

THE GUNSMITH by J. R. Roberts

Clint Adams was a legend among lawmen, outlaws, and ladies. They called him . . . the Gunsmith.

LONGARM by Tabor Evans

The popular long-running series about Deputy U.S. Marshal Custis Long—his life, his loves, his fight for justice.

SLOCUM by Jake Logan

Today's longest-running action Western. John Slocum rides a deadly trail of hot blood and cold steel.

BUSHWHACKERS by B. J. Lanagan

An action-packed series by the creators of Longarm! The rousing adventures of the most brutal gang of cutthroats ever assembled—Quantrill's Raiders.

DIAMONDBACK by Guy Brewer

Dex Yancey is Diamondback, a Southern gentleman turned con man when his brother cheats him out of the family fortune. Ladies love him. Gamblers hate him. But nobody pulls one over on Dex . . .

WILDGUN by Jack Hanson

The blazing adventures of mountain man Will Barlow—from the creators of Longarm!

TEXAS TRACKER by Tom Calhoun

J. T. Law: the most relentless—and dangerous—manhunter in all Texas. Where sheriffs and posses fail, he's the best man to bring in the most vicious outlaws—for a price.

TABOR EVANS

LONGARM

AND THE DIABLO GOLD

JOVE BOOKS, NEW YORK

THE BERKLEY PUBLISHING GROUP
Published by the Penguin Group
Penguin Group (USA) Inc.
375 Hudson Street, New York, New York 10014, USA

Penguin Group (Canada), 90 Eglinton Avenue East, Suite 700, Toronto, Ontario M4P 2Y3, Canada
(a division of Pearson Penguin Canada Inc.)
Penguin Books Ltd., 80 Strand, London WC2R 0RL, England
Penguin Group Ireland, 25 St. Stephen's Green, Dublin 2, Ireland (a division of Penguin Books Ltd.)
Penguin Group (Australia), 250 Camberwell Road, Camberwell, Victoria 3124, Australia
(a division of Pearson Australia Group Pty. Ltd.)
Penguin Books India Pvt. Ltd., 11 Community Centre, Panchsheel Park, New Delhi—110 017, India
Penguin Group (NZ), 67 Apollo Drive, Rosedale, North Shore 0632, New Zealand
(a division of Pearson New Zealand Ltd.)
Penguin Books (South Africa) (Pty.) Ltd., 24 Sturdee Avenue, Rosebank, Johannesburg 2196,
South Africa

Penguin Books Ltd., Registered Offices: 80 Strand, London WC2R 0RL, England

This is a work of fiction. Names, characters, places, and incidents either are the product of the author's imagination or are used fictitiously, and any resemblance to actual persons, living or dead, business establishments, events, or locales is entirely coincidental.

LONGARM AND THE DIABLO GOLD

A Jove Book / published by arrangement with the author

PRINTING HISTORY
Jove edition / May 2008

Copyright © 2008 by The Berkley Publishing Group.
Cover illustration by Miro Sinovcic.

ISBN: 978-0-515-14464-2

JOVE®
Jove Books are published by The Berkley Publishing Group,
a division of Penguin Group (USA) Inc.,
375 Hudson Street, New York, New York 10014.
JOVE is a registered trademark of Penguin Group (USA) Inc.
The "J" design is a trademark belonging to Penguin Group (USA) Inc.

PRINTED IN THE UNITED STATES OF AMERICA

10 9 8 7 6 5 4 3 2 1

Chapter 1

It was a fine summer afternoon, and most of the pedestrians strolling along Denver's Colfax Avenue were families enjoying the good weather and downtown shopping. Deputy United States Marshal Custis Long was on his way to his favorite saloon for billiards, beer, and boiled eggs when he saw a scuffle up ahead and then he heard screaming. Suddenly, a pair of pickpockets grabbed an old lady's black leather purse and knocked her off the sidewalk into the path of an onrushing freight wagon. A well-dressed man tried to grab and hold on to one of the thugs, but the other one slashed him across the throat with a knife.

Everyone panicked and many scattered in fear. Mothers scooped up their children and men stood frozen in shock. Someone, probably a doctor, knelt beside the man who'd had his throat slashed and frantically tried to save the man's life.

Longarm had learned to act instinctively, and that is why he was the only one on the sidewalk who didn't hesitate even for a moment, but instead jumped to the old

1

woman's aid. He was a tall, powerful man. So even though the old lady was heavyset, Longarm lifted her completely off the ground with one hand, and at the same time reached up and grabbed the bit of the wagon's lead horse and pushed the big animal just enough to the side. The huge iron-clad front wheel of the wagon missed crushing him and the helpless lady by inches.

"Whoa!" the driver shouted, hauling on the lines. "Whoa!"

Longarm and the woman toppled back on the sidewalk as the stunned crowd closed in around them offering help and advice. Everyone was upset, some crying in helpless anger.

"How is he?" Longarm asked the doctor treating the wounded man.

"His throat is cut, but not deep enough to have severed the jugular or the windpipe," the doctor answered in a terse voice as he tore open his medical kit. "I'll get the bleeding under control. He'll make it."

The old woman was dazed, but came around fast. "Are you all right, ma'am?"

"They stole my purse!" she cried. "I was carrying my life savings!"

Longarm brushed the dirt and grit off himself and climbed to his feet. He was tall enough to be able to look over the crowd and see the backs of the two pickpockets as they ran past the U.S. Mint with the old lady's purse in hand. One of them was wearing a red cap, and that clicked in Longarm's mind. "I recognize that pair," he growled. "And I know about where they're heading."

"Then get them!" the woman begged. "If I lose all

that money, I'll be destitute! Please, I'll pay you a reward!"

"Not necessary," he replied. "I'm a federal officer of the law."

"Then why are you still standing here? They're getting away!"

Longarm glanced down at the doctor and his bleeding patient, who was still losing a lot of blood. "It's a good thing you were close," he told the doctor a moment before he shouldered through the crowd and took off running after the fleeing pair.

He saw them round a street corner up ahead and disappear. But he knew that they were heading for the slums where they had friends and probably hiding places.

Longarm made quite a dashing figure as he ran after the pickpockets, and people all along the avenue stopped to stare. He was six four, well dressed in a brown suit, and his face was deeply tanned and craggy. He had a sweeping handlebar mustache and striking blue gray eyes. One pretty woman, on the arm of her escort, actually smiled and waved at Longarm as he flew past and rounded the street corner.

He was gaining on the pair, who were again in plain sight. Their names were Willard and Ernie, and Longarm had arrested them on numerous occasions for various petty crimes against both people and property. He had always known that they were thieves and criminals, but this was the first time they had stooped so low as to slash a man's throat and callously knock an old woman down in front of a wagon, not caring if she was run over and killed.

"This time you're *both* going to prison," Longarm

3

vowed out loud as he raced up the street after the pair that, until now, he had considered more of a nuisance than a real danger. No doubt they had been hanging around one of the major banks just hoping to see someone exit with plenty of cash. The old woman was an obvious and easy target. They must have followed her a block or two away from the bank and then made their bold and heartless move.

Every city that Longarm had ever visited had its slum section. These were the areas of a town that a man ventured into knowing full well that his gun had better be handy. These areas were always frequented by criminals, drunks, opium addicts, and prostitutes who preyed on each other as well as on any unsuspecting person who made the mistake of entering their realm. Denver's bad part of town was the equal of any that Longarm had ever seen. The area was so lawless that not a week passed without several murders being committed, often in broad daylight. He had never gone into this section unless duty required him to make an arrest. And now, as he entered the run-down maze of old homes and rooming houses, brothels, and bars, Longarm knew that he was on dangerous and unfamiliar ground.

The two thugs up ahead were unaware that they were being followed. Winded and feeling safe, they stopped to catch their breath. One opened the stolen purse, then grabbed a handful of cash. He began to hoot, and the other one joined him in coarse laughter—until they happened to notice Longarm racing toward them with his Colt .44-40 in his fist and his federal officer's badge glinting in the bright sunlight.

"Stop! You're under arrest!" Longarm bellowed.

The two men turned and ran into a nearby abandoned brick building, slamming the door behind them.

Longarm skidded to a halt outside the building and grabbed the rusty doorknob. To his surprise, it had been locked from the inside by the pair.

"Damn!" he swore.

Longarm reared back on one leg and kicked the door as hard as he could, hoping to tear it from its hinges. The door held.

He rushed to the closest window, which was already shattered. Longarm kicked again, and when the windowpane was completely broken out, he climbed inside a dim and rank-smelling room, then immediately stumbled over a drunk who muttered unintelligible curses.

Longarm found the door, then found himself in a hallway that might once have been elegant except for the fact that its ceiling was falling in and there were holes in its walls kicked or beaten in by angry, drunken men. He paused and listened. He heard the sound of running footsteps in the back of the building, and followed them through a maze of trashed rooms.

"Stop or I'll shoot!" he yelled at the two men as they blasted out the back of the building into an alley.

Longarm went after them. When he exited the old ruined building into the alley, he saw that the two men had run headlong into a trap they could not escape because of a mountain of rubble from a fallen-in brick wall.

"You're under arrest!" Longarm yelled, raising his gun.

The two men dove in behind a mound of bricks, and a moment later they opened fire.

5

Longarm dived back into the old building and took a moment to assess the situation. In the instant that he'd had to size up the back alley and decide that the pair were trapped, he'd also seen that getting to them would put him in terrible danger. They were not more than twenty yards distant, but how was he going to capture them without running straight into their line of fire?

"Damn," Longarm swore, bowing his head and concentrating hard. "There's no way I can get to them without getting hit unless they are the world's two worst shots."

He stuck his head out of the back doorway again, and a bullet ricocheted off the wall just inches from his head. He ducked back inside now, knowing that at least one of the pair could shoot straight.

A young lawman, bold and foolish, would have charged the pair and maybe killed them—but more likely have gotten himself killed. Longarm wasn't old, but neither was he young and foolish. He knew that Ernie and Willard were drunks, and he doubted that they had a bottle to give them comfort and courage. No, they had probably been so desperate for whiskey that they'd decided to snatch an old woman's purse in broad daylight. So now they had her money, but their thirst for liquor would be raging.

"I'll wait them out," he said to himself with a nod of approval. "Maybe they'll get desperate enough to surrender."

Longarm removed a five-cent cheroot from his vest pocket and lit it. He squatted down on his boot heels, tipped back his flat-brimmed hat, and made himself comfortable. He didn't think that Willard and Ernie

6

would last more than an hour or two, and then they'd give up both themselves and the poor woman's money.

An hour passed, and Longarm finished his cheroot and lit a second. All the while, he could hear the pair arguing behind their protective pile of brick rubble. The argument was getting more and more heated, and that told him that Willard and Ernie were getting mighty thirsty.

"Hey!" one of the pair finally yelled. "Who are you?"

"Deputy United States Marshal Custis Long."

There was a pause. "We got that old woman's money. We'll share it with you, Marshal. You can have a third and all you have to do is let us go free."

Longarm was not one to waste a lot of breath negotiating terms with thieves and cutthroats. "No dice."

Another pause, and then: "Marshal, we counted the money. It comes to six hundred and forty dollars! That means you'd get over two hundred. And who's to know you took your fair share?"

"I'd know," Longarm told them. "No deals. You boys slashed a man's throat just a while ago. You're going to jail, maybe even to prison."

"Gawdamn you, we didn't mean to do that! The fool I cut got in our way. Tried to be a damned Good Samaritan. Besides, I don't reckon he is going to die."

"Lucky for you," Longarm said, "or you'd both wind up swinging from the hangman's rope."

"We never meant to hurt anyone," the other man shouted. "We just need this damned money! Come on, Marshal! We'll never have another chance to get away with this much cash!"

"You won't," Longarm yelled.

Angry, the two men unleashed several shots at the doorway, but Longarm was far enough inside to be safe.

Another hour passed, and now the voices at the end of the alley sounded desperate and furious. Longarm waited patiently, thinking how it was a shame to have to spend so much time in this miserable building waiting for this pair to surrender. Maybe, if he did pretend to accept their offer, they would surrender. There was nothing wrong with backing out of a deal with a pair of rotten apples.

"Marshal!"

Longarm heard real desperation in the voice. "Yeah?"

"We'll give you . . . we'll give you *half*! That's over three hundred and twenty dollars, damn your eyes! Three hundred and twenty, Marshal! How long will it take you to earn that much money risking your life for that shiny badge? Use your head!"

Longarm patted his vest pocket and saw that he had no more cheroots to smoke, and even he was getting impatient and restless. "All right. You got a deal, boys!"

He could almost hear their happy sighs of relief.

"Throw down your gun, Marshal."

"Throw out yours first," Longarm replied, checking the double-barreled little hideout derringer that was affixed to his watch chain. The derringer wasn't the least bit accurate, but Longarm sure felt better for having it as backup. He wasn't forgetting that the two men had knives and weren't the least bit reluctant to use them.

"Marshal, how about we throw them out all together and stand up face-to-face?" one of the fugitives asked. "We're ready if you are."

"I'm more than ready," Longarm agreed, easing out of the doorway with his gun in his hand.

Ernie and Willard appeared, and moved cautiously around from behind their cover. Their guns were in their fists, and both men looked pale and shaky. Ernie was holding the old woman's purse up tight against his body.

"Okay," Willard said, dropping his gun. "Your turn, Marshal."

Longarm wanted to be closer so that, if push came to shove, he could put the derringer into action. He began walking toward the pair with his six-gun held loosely in his hand. Ernie was still clutching his gun.

"Drop it, Ernie. Drop it right now."

But the filthy man shook his head stubbornly. "It's *your* turn, Marshal. You drop yours right now."

Longarm was within fifteen feet of the pair. He could see that they were sweating and had the shakes. He crouched and laid his revolver on the ground, keeping it close to his hand. "Now you do the same, Ernie."

Instead of dropping his gun, Ernie raised it and fired. If he hadn't been in such a rush and so shaky from lack of alcohol, he'd have killed Longarm. But he was shaky and rushed, so his bullet went wild. Longarm snatched up his revolver and fired it just a foot off the ground. His bullet took an upward path and plowed through Ernie's forehead, killing him instantly.

Willard lunged forward screaming, and Longarm shot him through the throat. He took a few wobbly steps, then crashed facedown.

Longarm got the old woman's purse and turned his back on both of the dead men, muttering, "You boys should have surrendered peacefully. A year or two behind bars would have done wonders for your health and frame of mind."

He exited the alley, making a note to tell the local police about the two bodies. Then Longarm hiked back down the street, and found everyone gone except the old lady. When she saw her purse, she broke out in a big smile.

"Marshal, you did it! You saved me from destitution!"

"My pleasure, ma'am."

"I was beginning to think that you were *never* coming back. I heard a bunch of gunshots off in the distance. What happened to those two deadbeats who stole my purse?"

"They're off to the Promised Land," Longarm said.

The old woman grinned with satisfaction. "Well, the pearly gates of heaven won't open for them and that's for sure! If you ask me, they're burning in hell right now."

"Maybe they are," Longarm said, handing the woman her purse. "How was the man doing who tried to help you?"

"You mean that fool who got his throat cut?"

Longarm thought that was a rather harsh assessment of a man who'd tried to come to her aid, but he decided not to point out that fact. "That's the one."

"They hauled him off to the hospital. The doctor said he was going to live. He wanted to examine me, but I put the kibosh on that! Can you imagine?"

"I'm glad to hear that."

The woman opened her purse and slowly counted the money. "It's all here and you, Marshal, deserve a reward."

"Not necessary."

"Well, Marshal, if you insist," she said, smiling sweetly. "Have a good day."

He needed to offer her a warning. "Ma'am?"

"Yes?"

"If I were you, I'd get all that cash back in the bank just as soon as possible."

"I'm leaving today for San Francisco," she told him. "And this is my fare and my future in California."

"Do you have friends or relatives there?"

"Not a soul."

"Then why—"

She cut him off. "Marshal, I have lived my whole life hating cold winters and snow. No more of that for me. From now on it's the sea and sunshine. They say you can see whales passing San Francisco Bay. Can you imagine that!"

"Nope. But I sure wish you a lot of good luck. And do keep that money out of sight."

"You better believe I will. And I'm going to buy a gun right now to protect myself and my money from thieves and muggers. Bye, Marshal!"

Longarm stood and watched her walk down the street. His eyes happened to drop to the sidewalk and he saw a lot of fresh blood. Then, he glanced up at the clear blue sky and thought it was far too nice of a day for so much cutting and killing. Oh, well. A man had to take what misery and danger came his way and just make the best of it.

Longarm started off to the police station to alert them and file a report on the two dead men, and then he'd buy himself a few cigars and head over to the billiards hall. He had only lost an hour or so and he'd sure done his good deed for this fine day.

Chapter 2

Longarm got his cigars, but he never quite made it to the billiards parlor because he ran into Veronica Allan. She was an old flame who had moved down to Pueblo for a time, and now here she was back in Denver. Tall, with red hair and blue green eyes, Veronica was quite a looker, although Longarm had found her to be a little bossy.

"Why, if it isn't Marshal Custis Long!" Veronica exclaimed when they practically bumped into each other by accident right in front of the Colorado State Capitol Building.

"Veronica! How are you and what brings you back to town? I thought you were going to get married in Pueblo."

"Me, too," she said with a hint of disgust. "I thought I'd finally found the man I wanted to marry, but he turned out to be a worthless gambler. When he spent all of his money and then *my* money, I tried to find a good job in Pueblo, but never did. So I came back here where I've always been lucky. And my luck must be holding because here we are . . . together again."

Longarm almost laughed. "And do you think it was

13

luck or the fates that brought us together right here and now?"

"I don't know," she said, boldly looking him up and down. "You gave me a pretty good time, but then when I hinted that I'd like to get married, you dropped me like a hot potato."

"I told you right from the start that I've no intention of getting hitched," Longarm said, his smile slipping. "At least I was honest."

"Yeah," Veronica admitted, "you were. But I kept hoping I could change your mind."

"You gave it a good try," he admitted, "but you know the old saying about how you can lead a horse to water but you can't make it drink."

Veronica laughed. "You haven't changed a bit. Still living in those rooms over near Cherry Creek?"

"I am."

Veronica placed her arms around his neck. "Custis, could you do a friend a favor?"

"If I can."

Veronica sighed, and Longarm could see that she looked to be under some strain. "Custis, darling, to be honest, I'm dead broke. It took my last dollar to pay the fare up here from Pueblo, and I haven't the money to get a room or even a meal. I don't suppose that . . ."

"How much money do you need right now?"

"I'd rather not take your money," she said, looking embarrassed. "I was hoping that you . . ."

"Say no more," Longarm told her. "We'll go get a steak and a bottle and you can stay with me as long as you need to get a job and back on your feet. But I'm sure you remember that I only have one bed."

14

She winked and kissed his mouth. "Oh, yes, I remember. And that's the best part."

Longarm gave Veronica his arm and started down the street. "Are you pretty hungry?"

"Like a starved lion."

"Good," he said, "because where I'm taking you, the steaks are as big around as supper plates and two inches thick."

"Yummy," Veronica said. "I could eat the back end of a . . . oh, never mind. Let's hurry before I pass out from hunger."

They had a fine meal and then to walk it off, they strolled along the meandering path beside Cherry Creek. Longarm was enjoying the beautiful weather, but his mind kept going back to Ernie and Willard. True, they were worthless and heartless drunks, but he was still sorry that he'd had to kill them. Longarm had killed a lot of men, but most of them were truly bad people. Ernie and Willard, however, had seemed more pathetic than evil. They'd succumbed to the drink, and it had robbed them of their souls, and, ultimately, had cost them their lives. Longarm made a mental note to find out what paupers' graves they'd be buried in and then buy them small marble headstones. It wasn't much, but the gesture would ease his conscience a mite, and that was what was really important.

"You seem kind of distracted," Veronica said as they neared his rooms. "Are you thinking of another woman? Shoot, for all I know you're living with another woman."

"No, I'm not," Longarm said, before explaining how he'd had to gun down two muggers.

15

"If they pushed an old lady in front of a wagon and cut a man's throat, it sure doesn't seem to me like they had any breaks coming."

"I'm sure you're right. But I knew that pair from way back. One of them lost his family in a house fire and became a drunkard, and the other was beaten so savagely that he was partially deranged. Over the years, they became friends and followed the same downhill path. I guess they finally got so desperate and crazed for liquor that they hit bottom."

"If they lived such tormented lives, perhaps they are better off dead."

"I doubt they'd think so," Longarm replied. "And anyway, it just seems like too nice of a day to have had to shoot anyone. Maybe I'm just tired of killing. Or maybe I'm just feeling a little down in the dumps."

"I know a cure for that," Veronica said, her hand dropping down to brush his thigh. "And I think I'm just what the doctor would have ordered for you."

He had to grin. "Veronica, you're probably right, and I think we ought to go upstairs to my rooms and find out."

Longarm wasted no time in locking his door, pulling the shades, and undressing. Veronica wasn't slow about disrobing either. Within minutes, they were tumbling on the bed, kissing and caressing.

Longarm pounced on Veronica the way a hungry mountain lion might pounce on a helpless deer. Veronica bit his neck and then struggled, pretending to try to fight him off. But Longarm's blood and rod were both up, and he pinned her to his bed and then impaled her with a deep thrust.

"Oh!" Veronica cried, her eyes widening as if she had never before known a man. "Oh . . . oh, don't . . . don't stop!"

Longarm had no intention of stopping. Veronica's eyes squeezed shut, and the tip of her tongue poked out from between her lips. Each time Longarm plunged his manhood in and out of her honey pot, she gasped with heightened pleasure.

"Harder," she moaned. "Harder!"

Longarm was more than happy to oblige the lady, who was now wrapping her long legs around his waist and pumping furiously. He felt like a stallion, and knew that he was carrying a big, wet load.

"I want on top now," she finally whispered. "Please!"

Longarm rolled over on his back and let the woman sit on her lovely haunches and bounce up and down on his stiff rod. Veronica's eyes were open again, but glazed with pleasure. Her head was thrown back and her hair was waving back and forth to the rhythm of their love-making like sea grass waving in a storm.

"Oh, Custis," she breathed, "I could do this for hours!"

"I couldn't," he said with a laugh as he finally rolled back on top of Veronica and rode her roughshod, sucking on her nipples until even she had had enough. "Are you ready?" he asked in a hoarse voice.

"I'm comin'! I'm comin'!"

Longarm felt her begin to quiver, and then he shut off her scream of pleasure as he filled her with his great reservoir of hot seed.

When they were finished, they lay panting and smiling.

"We haven't lost a thing in bed," Veronica told him. "You're still the best I ever had."

"We're incredible together," he fully agreed.

"We could be good together a lot more," she said. "I wish that—"

"Don't say anything more," Longarm gently suggested. "Let's just enjoy ourselves day by day and let things unfold without being forced."

She nodded and snuggled closer to him. "Tomorrow I'm going to find a good job. And when I get my first paycheck, I'm going to buy you something special for taking me in and feeding me."

"I *like* feeding you," he told her with a wink, then added, "Feeding you what's hanging between my legs."

Veronica giggled. "Yes, that's the best feeding you could give me. But I still want to buy you a special present."

"I don't need anything special."

Veronica leaned over and kissed his lips. "I don't care what you say. You're getting a present from me that you'll long remember."

"I just got one I'll long remember."

Veronica snuggled in tight against his body. "Custis, I sure hope that they don't send you on another dangerous assignment for a while."

"Me, too," Longarm said. "Right after you left for Pueblo, I had a job in Montana. I was gone for a month and got caught in a blizzard up in the mountains. Had to track down and kill a gunfighter for hire."

Veronica pushed up on her elbows and studied his face with concern. "A professional?"

"Yeah," Longarm said, remembering. "A gunman

18

who hired out for the highest dollar and who I knew without doubt would kill his best friend if the money was right."

"How did you manage to kill such a dangerous man?"

Longarm was quiet for a few moments before he answered. "I knew that he was probably faster than me with a gun. He had a well-established reputation for his speed and accuracy with a Colt. So on the day that I knew I'd have to face the man, I borrowed a sawed-off double-barreled shotgun. I came upon Harry Drago after he'd been up drinking all night and was shaky. I told him he was under arrest. When Drago went for his gun, I just flipped up the barrels of that shotgun and pulled both triggers."

Veronica waited, finally saying, "And?"

Longarm shook his head and felt revulsion. "I shot Harry Drago higher than I'd expected."

Veronica leaned closer, drawn by morbid fascination. "You mean that the shotgun blasts hit the gunfighter in the head?"

"Yeah," Longarm confessed. "The blasts tore Drago's head and neck right off his shoulders like a guillotine would have done, only my method was a whole lot messier."

Veronica flopped back on the mattress and stared at the ceiling. After a long silence, she said, "I don't know how you do things like that, Custis. I know that you were in the Civil War and saw all kinds of horror . . . but now you're back doing . . ."

Longarm placed his forefinger over her newly bruised and ruby red lips. "Why don't we talk about something else?" he suggested. "Like what we are going to do tonight or tomorrow."

Veronica looked relieved. "Good idea! As for tonight, we're going to screw our brains out. But tomorrow, you're going back to work and I'm going out on the town to look for work."

"Where will you start looking?"

"I don't know," she admitted, her brow furrowing in thought. "I don't want to work the saloons anymore. I want to come home evenings and cook for you and then make love by candlelight or moonlight from your bedroom's window."

Longarm thought a moment, and then he had a splendid idea. "I have a friend who owns a dress shop. A very successful dress shop. You'd be perfect there and well paid and treated."

"How do you know this woman?"

"It's not a woman." Longarm chuckled to himself. "Actually, Veronica, the owner is a *man*."

"How odd that a man would sell women's dresses!"

"Well," Longarm said, "this man is a little different from most. Quite different actually."

Veronica blinked with surprise as she realized what Longarm was implying. "And *you* know him?"

"Yeah," Longarm said. "I saved his boyfriend's life a while ago. The poor man was being savagely beaten by some bullies. After I stepped in and helped, both of them regarded me as their big guardian angel. They are nice fellows and we have a clear understanding of our differences."

Veronica nodded. "How strange that a man like you would befriend people like that."

"I hate bullies," Longarm told her. "And I hate cruel and stupid injustice. The man that I'm going to send you to is a very decent human being, just odd. You'll like him, Veronica. And I think he'll like you."

Veronica shrugged. "Well, I've never been around that kind, so it'll be an experience."

"Just treat Victor and his friend Jessie like you would any other two nice people, and everything will work out fine."

Veronica gave that some thought, but soon her interest turned back to Longarm's body. And without a word, she began to caress his manhood back into a towering, throbbing erection.

Maybe, Longarm thought as he eagerly mounted the woman, Veronica just needed to get her thoughts about men back to more familiar ground.

Chapter 3

Longarm went to work the next day at the U.S. marshal's office near the Denver Mint. It was a fine day as he entered the Federal Building, and Irma, the attractive receptionist on the ground floor, greeted him with more than her usual loud hello. She patted her glossy hair and smoothed the bodice of her nicest dress.

"Why, Marshal Long," she said, smiling broadly and pointing at the morning edition of Denver's most popular newspaper. "Congratulations! You made our newspaper's front page again. I read here that you shot and killed two muggers after saving an old lady and some poor bugger who got his throat slashed for interfering on her behalf."

Longarm was not in the habit of reading the morning paper until after he'd had a cup of coffee at his office desk. And he wasn't pleased about making the front page because he had too many enemies in Denver and liked to stay out of their minds and gun sights.

"Well," Irma challenged, "aren't you going to tell me it's all true?"

"I didn't know the damned story was going to be front-page news."

"You're Denver's everyday hero and everything you do seems to draw a lot of attention."

"That's never been my intention," Longarm said defensively. "This time, I really tried to get the pair of thieves to surrender, but they decided they'd rather shoot it out. Fatal mistake on their part, Irma."

"Obviously," she said, winking. "Custis, how many gunfights have you been in so far just this year?"

"Too many," Longarm told her, not wanting to discuss the matter as other employees were entering the building, some stopping to eavesdrop.

"You must have a *big* gun," Irma said, eyes dropping to Longarm's crotch. "I'd just love to see it sometime. Sometime real soon."

Longarm blushed, knowing that Irma sure as hell wasn't talking about his Colt revolver. Several of his coworkers overheard Irma's salacious remark and tittered. Irma was known as being man-hungry and easy. In fact, Longarm had lost count of the number of men in his own office that she'd readily hopped into bed with. He also knew that she'd had to be treated for gonorrhea, and that was another reason he avoided her like the plague. But the slatternly Irma seemed to have him at the top of her conquest list, and the woman's bold persistence was really starting to grate on Longarm.

"Well, big boy," Irma said, obviously enjoying his discomfort, "when are you going to show that big shooter of yours to me?"

If they had been alone, Longarm might have unbuttoned his pants and waved his large salami at her, but he was a gentleman and not at all in the habit of insulting women. Still, Irma had gone too far this time, so he said, "Irma, to be honest, the only reason that I haven't already shown it to you is that I like to keep my big shooter clean and in good working order."

Irma flushed bright red, and two men who had overheard the exchange broke out in gales of ribald laughter. Longarm didn't rub it in because Irma was already thoroughly humiliated, so he just tipped his hat to the woman and headed upstairs to his office.

"Nice comeback!" Melvin Dorfman said, hurrying after him. "You really gave it to her this morning. I didn't think anyone could embarrass that hussy, but you sure did."

"I wish that she'd just do her job and quit bothering me," Longarm said with irritation.

Dorfman caught Longarm's sleeve and whispered, "Say, old friend. Do you think she's still got the clap? Has her doctor cleared her or—"

Longarm shook his head, disgusted by the question. "Melvin, I don't know and I don't care."

"Well, I sure do," Dorfman said. "I'm real interested in getting a taste of Irma. I've heard that she is a wildcat in bed. A real ball-bustin' whang-danger that will gladly suck the—"

"Melvin," Longarm growled in anger, "shut the hell up! If you want to strap on Irma, then I'm sure you can do it for the price of a lousy dinner and a bottle of cheap wine. But spare me the sordid details. Understand?"

"Hey," Melvin said as they entered their office, "you don't have to get snappy with me. I was just talking, you know."

"I know," Longarm growled, "and that seems to be what you do best around here. Talk."

"Hey, screw you!" Melvin snorted in anger. "You shoot two drunks over the weekend and give an old lady back her money, and maybe you think that makes you better than the rest of us. Well, it don't."

Longarm felt a powerful need to grab Melvin Dorfman by the throat and shake the shit out of him. Instead, he managed to say, "Right. Now go find something to do and leave me alone."

"Screw you!"

Longarm started to go for the man's throat, but he noticed that his boss was frantically motioning him to come join him in his office. "Melvin," Longarm said, wanting to give the man his parting shot, "I think you should go tell Irma that you want to take her out to dinner and then to bed. I'll bet she'll just jump at your invitation and give you a night you will never forget."

"Maybe I will ask her," Melvin Dorfman said, turning to go back down the stairs.

"Perfect," Longarm called down at the man. "Because that means you'll wind up needing medical leave and I won't have to listen to your garbage every day around the coffeepot."

"Hey, screw you!" Melvin yelled, loud enough to be heard clear out in the lobby of the Federal Building.

Longarm shook his head with disgust because Melvin Dorfman was an idiot and completely worthless in the field. As far as Longarm could tell, the man did very little other than shuffle papers, gossip about loose women, and make coffee for people who actually worked. Melvin was the son of some very high-ranking Washington, D.C., bureaucrat, and everyone in the building knew that was the only reason Dorfman still had a job.

"Custis, come on in and close the door," Marshal Billy Vail said from behind his polished dark walnut desk.

Longarm closed the door and took a seat. Billy moved a few papers around on his desk and then said, "Have you had coffee yet?"

"Not enough."

Billy went to the door, opened it, and called out to Melvin to bring them two cups on the double.

"Dorfman is down in the lobby asking Irma to go out tonight."

"What?"

"That's right."

"Doesn't he know that she—"

"I think he knows, but can't help himself," Longarm explained. "You ought to get rid of that guy. He's poison around here. Doesn't carry his weight and creates lots of problems in the office."

"I know," Billy said, trying to make light of the touchy subject, "but Dorfman does make one helluva good pot of coffee."

"He's an absolute disgrace to the badge," Longarm said with his typical bluntness.

"He's also got a lot of high-powered connections in Washington close to my top boss," Billy replied, picking up the morning newspaper and pointing at the front-page story concerning Longarm's heroism. "So let's forget about firing Mr. Dorfman right now and talk about your exciting and newsworthy weekend."

"I haven't read that article," Longarm said. "What does it say?"

27

"Just that you saved an old lady from being crushed by an onrushing freight wagon, risking your life in the process. That true?"

Longarm shrugged. "More or less."

"More, I'd bet," Billy said. "And also that you probably saved the life of a Mr. Sylvester Potts, who had his throat slashed."

"That's *not* true," Longarm disagreed. "The wound wasn't fatal and there was a doctor immediately on hand. There was a lot of blood and hysterics, but Potts would have survived even without a doctor."

"All right," Billy conceded, "so you only saved one life, not two."

"Correct."

"Did you know the identities of those two muggers that you gunned down in the alley?"

"I didn't gun them down," Longarm countered a little defensively. "I did everything I could to get them to surrender, but no dice. They offered me money from the old woman's purse, and I finally agreed to take it."

Billy's eyebrows shot up. "You did?"

"Yes, but only to get them to drop their weapons and come out so that I could make the arrest."

"So what went wrong?"

"They got stupid," Longarm said, putting it as simply as he could. "They tried to kill me, so I ran out of options and killed them first."

"Did you know that one of the dead men, a Mr. Willard Weatherford, was once a man of some position and importance?"

"Yes." Longarm shrugged. "Tragic story of a man

who was ruined by personal misfortune and turned in his sorrows to drink."

"Yes," Billy agreed. "The trouble is that Mr. Weatherford does have some friends in the mayor's office. And now, they are demanding a full-scale investigation of the shooting."

"What!" Longarm was outraged. "Listen, Billy, Weatherford and his thieving friend were seen by dozens of people on the street not a block from here. They shoved the old woman into the path of that freight wagon and slashed a man's throat. What's to investigate?"

Billy threw up his hands. "I know. I know. It's ridiculous, but just once I wish you could simply arrest or apprehend someone instead of shooting them to death."

Longarm was getting pissed off. First, Irma with her smart mouth had embarrassed him in front of people. Then, Melvin with his dirty mouth had offended him. Now, his friend and boss was saying that he should have handled the situation in that filthy back alley differently.

Longarm came to his feet. "Billy," he said, "you need to back me up all the way on this because I did *nothing* wrong."

"They were just a sorry pair of petty thieves and drunks," Billy said, avoiding Longarm's eyes.

"Yeah," Longarm shot back. "And they'd obviously gotten to the point where they were willing to kill for money that would buy them liquor. So when they crossed that line, I did the public a favor."

"Sit down," Billy said quietly. "You know I'll go to the wall for you on this with the mayor and that bunch.

29

But sometimes, just *once* perhaps, I wish you'd make an arrest so that the criminal went to court before a judge and jury. Okay?"

Longarm's dander was up. "Fine!"

"Custis, simmer down. I want you to write out a full report on the shooting. Don't read today's newspaper article first. Just sit down and write exactly what happened in that back alley. Then, I'll take your written report to the mayor's office, along with some of my comments on your behalf, and I'll cover your ass on this shooting all the way down the line."

"Thanks," Longarm said, meaning it as he relaxed. "You know, I really like being a marshal and doing my job, but sometimes the politics turn my stomach enough to make me want to hand in my badge and find another profession."

"Don't ever do that," Billy said with emphasis. "You're the finest lawman I have, and I know that you have integrity and courage. If I lost you, there simply wouldn't be any way to find your equal as a replacement."

Longarm almost smiled. "Damn your flattery, Billy. You should have been a politician."

"I *am* one."

Longarm realized it was sad but true. Once, Billy had been a deputy marshal just like himself, and a very good one. But with a family and needing more money to support a growing number of good children, Billy had climbed the promotional ladder right into a desk job that was always afloat in city, state, and federal politics.

"I hope it's worth all the money you make for the politics and crap you have to put up with in your job," Longarm said.

30

"It isn't," Billy admitted, "but I've got a lot of mouths to feed and I want my boys to go to a university and become successful and important enough to support me and my wife in our dotage."

"I get it," Longarm said, coming back to his feet. "And I'll write that report even though you know that writing is not what I do best."

"Just do it and I'll take care of the rest," Billy promised. "And when you finish, come back in here and I'll tell you about a very special job that I have for you in the New Mexico Territory."

Longarm smiled, spirits lifting. "You're sending me off again?"

"If you want."

Longarm grinned. "I want. But give me a day or two first."

"Why? Another woman?"

"Yeah," Longarm admitted. "One I haven't quite quenched my hunger for yet."

Billy scoffed. "Custis, whether you agree or not, sometimes you're worse than Dorfman."

"No, I'm not," Longarm said, turning serious. "Because I don't dip my wick in every dirty hole I can find and then tell the world about it like I was some kind of conquering hero."

"Let's not get back on the subject of Dorfman," Billy said. "Go write that report, and then we'll talk about a really important murder case I want you to handle in New Mexico. If you want this case, I can only give you till tomorrow to catch the train because this is far too hot to put on the back burner."

"Sounds *real* good," Longarm told his boss.

31

Chapter 4

It took a while for Longarm to write the shooting report, but not because he was illiterate or not well read. It just took time to really put it all down in a way that would be acceptable to Billy Vail as well as the city's local law officials. He had to justify killing Willard and Ernie, and the hard part of it was that there hadn't been any witnesses to the actual shooting, which had taken place in a dim and rubbish-filled alley.

"You're not writing the great American novel," Dorfman offered with a snicker. "Just the usual shoot-and-kill report that you have done so often that it's becoming boringly repetitive."

"Shut up," Longarm snapped at the man, "or I'll yank down your britches and write the whole report on your bare ass while everyone in the office dies laughing."

Dorfman's eyes widened in alarm and he left in a hurry. Longarm finished the report, and read it over twice to make sure it was exactly as he wanted. Satisfied, he took the report into Billy's office and laid it on the man's desk.

"There it is. As complete and accurate as I can make it," Longarm told the man.

Billy slowly read the report, occasionally nodding in agreement, all the way through. Then he looked up across his desk and said, "Custis, this will do perfectly."

"How about we talk about New Mexico?" Longarm asked.

Billy laid the report aside. "Sure. Let's put the past in the past concerning these shootings. The main thing is that I'd like you out of Denver and on your way to New Mexico no later than tomorrow."

"I'd like an extra day."

"Sorry, but it would be far better if you left tomorrow. That way, you won't be around to answer any questions about the shootings. And by the time you return to Denver, the deaths of Willard and Ernie will be history and no one will be on your back about why you couldn't arrest that pair without killing them."

"Fine," Longarm conceded. "If it's that important, then I'll leave on the train tomorrow. So what's the new assignment?"

Billy leaned back in his chair and gazed up at the ceiling for a moment to collect and arrange his thoughts and words. "Custis, do you remember reading about a sensational string of mysterious murders that took place down in Montezuma, New Mexico, this spring?"

"No."

"They involved that town's mayor, marshal, and two city councilmen. Surely you must have read—"

"No, I didn't read about them. I was probably off somewhere far away killing more bad men for you."

"Well, let me bring you up to date on them," Billy

34

said, leaning even farther back in his chair and lacing his hands behind his head. "There's been a string of political murders in Montezuma dating back to earlier this year."

"Political murders?" Longarm asked impatiently.

"First, the mayor of Montezuma died. He was shot to death in his office one evening. No witnesses. Then, the city councilman who was first in line for the mayor's job had a strange accident of some sort. He was struck down by a stray bullet, I think."

Longarm's eyebrows arched in question. "A 'stray bullet,' you say?"

"Yes. There was a shooting match and this city councilman, who was about to assume the office of mayor, was walking nearby and was hit in the head by a stray bullet and died instantly."

"Sounds pretty fishy to me," Longarm said, taking out a cheroot and biting off the tip, but not lighting it in Billy's office because the man didn't appreciate the smoke and aroma of cheap cigar tobacco.

"Yes, according to the newspaper accounts, everyone else in Montezuma thought it a little fishy, too. But still, no connections were made and no one thought overly much about it at the time. Just real bad luck, they all said, according to what I read."

"But then a second city councilman died?"

"Yes," Billy replied, his expression turning grave. "The unfortunate man was driving a buggy down to Taos on official business when he disappeared. When a search was undertaken, the mayor-to-be and his buggy were found in a deep ravine along with his dead horse. Apparently, they had had an accident and just went over the side of a cliff, plunging to their deaths."

35

Longarm shook his head. "It could happen. Does happen, but . . ."

"I know," Billy said, "but after the death of a mayor, and then the *two* senior city councilmen in line to become the new mayor . . . well, everyone was starting to ask a lot of questions. Yet, looking back at each of the deaths, there were no obvious suspects or motives."

"The obvious suspect would be the third city councilman who did become the mayor," Longarm said without hesitation. "I don't even have to go to Montezuma to figure that one out."

"Sure," Billy told him. "However, here is the kicker to that theory: When his turn came up to be mayor, the man declined! Yep, he refused to become mayor, and even resigned from the city council claiming that he didn't want to be the next future mayor to have an inexplicable and violent death."

Longarm frowned. "This is all pretty strange. Did you say that a marshal also died?"

"Unfortunately, I did." Billy leaned forward intently. "Here's the thing about that. The marshal died in a saloon, but nobody knows who killed him."

"I don't understand."

"Me neither," Billy said. "But from what little information I have from the *Montezuma Weekly News,* it seems that there was a drunken brawl in a Montezuma saloon called the Silver Spur. Fists were flying, chairs and tables were smashed, and then someone started shooting out the lights. When the wild melee was over and someone lit candles, the marshal lay dead on the floor with a knife protruding out of his back."

"And no one had any idea who did it?"

36

"Nope."

"What else?" Longarm asked, growing troubled.

Billy shrugged. "That's about the size of it. The remaining members of the town council all quit out of fear for their lives. The citizens are planning to elect a new mayor and town council, and they are still trying to find a new marshal. So far, there have been no takers for any of those offices."

"So who holds the power in Montezuma?"

"I don't know." Billy steepled his hands. "Have you ever heard of that town?"

"Sure. I've even been through it a few years ago. Nice town with a plaza and a very colorful history involving gold, silver, and cattle ranches. As I recall, there are some pretty wealthy people living in Montezuma and it's about halfway between Taos and Santa Fe."

"You've got it right," Billy said. "Montezuma is where some of the wealthiest men in New Mexico call home. Some of them are politicians who regularly go to Santa Fe on government business or to promote their special interests."

Longarm rolled the cheroot around in his mouth, then inspected it for a moment before saying, "Why do you think all these killings are so important and quite possibly related?"

"I have no real idea," Billy admitted. "Just operating on a hunch, I think, that it must have something to do with money and important territorial politics."

Longarm almost laughed out loud. "That's not too astute, Billy. And even worse, it's no help at all as far as trying to uncover the motive for all those murders."

"I know," Billy confessed. "I know. And here's

another very important complication. Vice President Chester Arthur is going to Santa Fe next month on an official visit. My bosses—*and yours*—are worried sick that the people who are behind all those murders in Montezuma might also try to assassinate the vice president."

Longarm blinked with surprise. "For what possible purpose?"

"That's for you to find out," Billy said. "And if there is no threat to the vice president, then we want to know that well before he arrives. However, if there is a threat, we have to eliminate it completely before the vice president's arrival."

"Why doesn't he just decide to not visit Santa Fe?" Longarm asked.

Billy made a face and then laughed without humor. "Fine idea! Why don't you tell Vice President Arthur not to go to Santa Fe? And when he asks why, you tell him you don't know, but some people in Montezuma have died mysteriously and there might be some kind of connection. See how far that gets you in public service, Custis. Hell, we'd both be fired if you pulled that stupid stunt."

Longarm saw the man's point. "Okay, Billy, but I sure don't want to try to get to the bottom of all these killings and at the same time be worried about the life of the vice president. He will have some federal protection, won't he?"

"Not a lot because he's only the vice president. My guess is that he'll have a few personal bodyguards. Two, perhaps three at the most."

"That's not many."

"No, it isn't," Billy agreed. "And you do know that

President James A. Garfield has already hinted that he will only serve one term, and that he will then expect the vice president to be elected for the next term."

Longarm caught the important implication in Billy's words. Someone in New Mexico might be interested in changing the course of American history by assassinating the man most likely to be the next president of the United States.

"Damn," Longarm said, feeling the enormous weight and responsibility of the assignment come crashing down on his broad shoulders. "This could be something really big."

"I know," Billy agreed. "And I'm counting on you to get to the bottom of things before the vice president arrives next month. We simply can't take the chance that there is some kind of political conspiracy taking place in the northern New Mexico Territory."

"I'll do my best to get to the bottom of things. But you and I both know that the string of murders in Montezuma might have absolutely nothing to do with the vice president's upcoming visit."

"I certainly hope that is true," Billy said. "But if there is even a remote possibility, then we have to investigate it and rule it out once and for all."

"I'll need more than my usual travel funds for this one," Longarm said, coming to his feet.

"You always say that," Billy groused. "Why is it that you expect to travel in such fine style?"

"Because I work better when I'm in nice surroundings," Longarm said. "If I have to stay in hovels, then I worry about getting robbed or murdered in my sleep. If I haven't the money to eat in the best places, I run the

39

risk of getting bad food poisoning. Would you rather have me shitting my insides out—or trying to make sure that the vice president is not next on some assassin's list?"

"Dammit, Custis, I—"

Longarm cut him off. "Now I ask you, Boss. Is saving a few government dollars worth me taking those risks when what I'm going to do in New Mexico might very well affect the course of America's history?"

Billy snorted and shook his head. "Custis, you're a real piece of work. Do you know that?"

"I've been told that I am—a few times. Mostly by you, but also by some of the women I've known."

"I'll just bet you have."

"I'll need three hundred dollars in cash when I leave tomorrow."

"Three hundred!"

"That's right."

"And how did you come up with that monstrous sum?"

"I mean to travel first class on the railroad, and I'll need money to pay informants and snitches. If I grease enough palms well enough in Montezuma, I can probably find out if all those killings were related or not. And I definitely want to find out who stabbed the marshal to death after the lights went out in that saloon." Longarm shrugged. "Surely, you understand that this is a professional issue between officers of the law."

"How about I requisition two hundred and send you more as needed?"

Longarm folded his muscular arms across his chest and shook his head. "Nope."

40

Billy flushed with anger, but it was gone in a moment. "All right, you big sonofabitch, you win."

"Thanks," Longarm said, unfolding his arms and coming to his feet. "Oh, and Billy. Understand that three hundred is in *addition* to my first-class round-trip ticket."

Billy started to protest, but Longarm was already heading out the door. He had many things to do before heading off to the New Mexico Territory and a string of murders that might very well lead to a plot to assassinate the vice president of the United States.

Chapter 5

Miss Veronica Allan bought a bottle of champagne because she felt like celebrating tonight. On Longarm's recommendation and despite some reservations, she'd gone to Victor's dress shop to see about a job. Victor, a tall, thin man in his thirties with a girlish giggle and a good sense of humor, had immediately taken Veronica into his confidence.

"I like dresses and pretty things," he'd confessed, "but I *don't* like uppity old women and they're usually the ones with the money."

"Then why don't you sell out?" Veronica had asked after seeing an inventory that was chic and fashionable, although a little on the expensive side.

"Well," Victor had admitted, "the truth is, this business makes a lot of money. And I haven't figured out anything that would do nearly as well financially. But I need a woman who can handle those irritating well-to-do old biddies. You know, someone who can charm their girdles off and make them feel like they actually look good in these dresses and gowns. Could you do that?"

"I believe that I could," Veronica had said truthfully. "At least, I'd sure be willing to give it a try."

Victor had clapped his hands, and then his friend Jessie had waltzed in the door, and they'd all three hit it off amazingly well. Veronica got the job with a fine starting salary plus a commission that she felt would make her more money than she'd ever made in saloons, where she'd always done quite well. And the hours were perfect, so she wouldn't be up half the night trying to fight off amorous men who were way too deep in their cups.

Yes, Veronica thought, it was perfect. Victor had even suggested that, in time if things worked out, he might be willing to sell the dress shop to her on an attractive payment plan. He and Jessie were thinking about relocating to New York City where a citizenry that was far more tolerant was to be found.

Longarm had given Veronica the key to his rooms, and she let herself in while humming a tune. She had an armful of groceries and the champagne, which she planned to put on ice. She'd cook Longarm a fine meal and after the champagne, they would make mad, passionate love. The only sad thought in her mind was that he could be leaving on an assignment at any time.

"Well," she said to herself, "maybe I can screw him into changing his profession. Getting on with the local law officers here or even the fire department. He'd do very well at either, I'm sure. Then, if I had the dress shop going well and making us good money, and he had a steady job in the fire or police department, we could buy a house, have some children, and live happily every after!"

These were Veronica's happy thoughts as she unpacked the groceries and thought about making dinner, while totally forgetting that she had forgotten to close the door.

She heard the man before she had time to even turn around, and by then it was too late. He was knocking her down and leaping on top of her, the stench of his awful breath and unwashed body immediately overwhelming her senses. Veronica tried to cry out in alarm, but he struck her with his closed fist and she spiraled into unconsciousness.

When Veronica awoke, she felt as if her head had exploded. She tasted blood in her mouth and one of her eyes was swollen completely shut. She moaned, and realized that her mouth had been filled with a gag, she was still on the kitchen floor, and her hands were tied tightly behind her back.

"So you're coming around, are you?" he said, leaning over to mock her.

Veronica wanted to vomit and she felt dizzy. One-eyed, she stared at the filthy man, wondering if he was going to kill or rape her. Then she looked down at herself to see if she had already been raped while unconscious. She hadn't been, and that was a huge relief.

"Who the hell are you?" the man asked as if she wasn't gagged and could actually reply. "You must be the lawman's wife or girlfriend, huh?"

Veronica sat up and when she tried to stand, she almost fell over. The stranger grabbed and shoved her into a chair. He was a big man, bearded, unwashed, and with a terrible scar down the side of his face from eyebrow to jawline.

"You're probably wondering what I'm going to do with you," he said, obviously amused by his own question. "That's what you're wondering, right?"

She nodded.

"Well, I haven't decided yet. Maybe after I kill Marshal Long, we can have a little fun in his bed. How would that be?"

Veronica's eyes filled with tears.

"Aw, don't cry! I won't kill you. Not as long as you treat me the way I want to be treated."

She recognized hunger in his bloodshot eyes and recoiled. He came over to her and roughly cupped one of her large breasts, saying, "I can't wait to see 'em when you're undressed. I'd do it to you right now, except that Marshal Long might come barging in on us, and I don't think he'd be too happy to find me humping his woman. Now would he?"

Veronica shook her head, feeling a rising sense of fear and panic.

"So I'm going to wait until he comes home to you, sweetie, and then I'm going to catch him by surprise and put my knife so deep in his belly that it'll come out his back. I'm going to skewer him like a stuck hog for what he done to Ernie and his friend Willard yesterday. He shot them down like dirty dogs in that alley, and didn't even wait for the undertaker to arrive. Just turned his back on their bodies like they were sacks of shit."

The man was getting worked up, and he took a huge bowie knife out of its sheath and waved it before Veronica's one good eye. "I'm going to stick Marshal Long good, and then I'm going to gag him like I did you and peel the hide off him while he dies screaming."

46

The man began to laugh uproariously. "And if there's time, before he dies, he's gonna watch me spread your legs and hump you until you holler! Ha! Ha!"

Veronica trembled from head to toe because now she knew what the man was going to do and that he was completely insane.

He forgot her for a moment. "I'm thirsty! What do you have good to drink in this place?"

Not expecting an answer, the man looked around and his eyes fell on the bottle of champagne. "Oh, my, oh, my!" he crowed. "Now ain't this something fancy! Champagne, and I'll bet it's good stuff, too! You and Marshal Custis Long were planning a little celebration, huh? Maybe he got a raise or promotion for shooting poor Ernie and Willard to death, the bastard."

The man grabbed the bottle, twisted out the cork, and brought the bottle to his lips. He poured the champagne into the hairy hole that was his mouth, and drank while the champagne ran down his whiskers onto the floor. He drank and drank until the entire bottle was empty, and then he belched, staggered back, and laughed like an idiot before collapsing onto Longarm's sofa.

"Damn! This is gonna be my celebration! And you, pretty woman, are going to be the icing on the cake. Yes, missy, I am going to take you like Sherman did the South! Ravage you right down to your bones and make you beg for mercy!"

Veronica couldn't help the tears that began to flood down her cheeks. Seeing them, he laughed even harder.

"I'll bet your hero has more liquor in this kitchen somewhere," the man said, tearing open cupboards until he found Longarm's bottle of good bourbon. "Yes, yes!"

He didn't bother with a glass, but instead swilled some of the bourbon down and then laughed some more.

Drink it all! Drink the whole bottle, you swine! Veronica thought. *Drink yourself into a drunken stupor and then see who is going to pay when Custis opens that door and sees what you've done to me, you animal!*

But the man did not drink the bottle. Instead, he wiped his lips and beard with his filthy sleeve, and then corked the bottle and replaced it in the cupboard. He winked and looked at Veronica. "You're hopin' I'll get drunk and pass out or something so that the lawman will find and kill me. That's what you're hopin', isn't it?"

Veronica shook her head desperately.

"Liar!" he snarled, the grin replaced by something terrible to behold. "You think you're so smart? Well, wait until the lawman is layin' on his back with my pig-sticker in his gizzard! And then when I skin his face while he gurgles and drowns on his own gore. Then you'll see who is smart and who isn't!"

He came over to her, grabbed the top of her dress, and ripped it apart, exposing her large, bare breasts. She tried to kick him in the crotch, but missed, and he laid his mouth on her breast and sucked loudly for a moment while she tried to fight. Then he hit her again so hard, she went to the floor and pretended to pass out.

"You're gonna be fun," he said, standing over her and roughly massaging her breasts for a moment before moving away.

Veronica wanted to scream, but she knew that he would only attack her again. *No,* she thought, *I'll wait until Custis starts to open the door, and then I'll do whatever it takes to warn him that a monster is hiding and waiting inside with a big knife clenched in his dirty hand.*

Longarm knew that Veronica wasn't going to be happy that he was leaving on the train tomorrow. But there was nothing he could do to change that fact, and so he'd tell her after drinks, dinner, and a rowdy bout of vigorous lovemaking. Veronica would be disappointed, but she would understand. And maybe she had gotten hired at the dress shop. If so, that would give her something to look forward to, and maybe it would even offer her a promising future. Victor had told him that he needed a pretty, fashionable, and attractive young woman to handle difficult but wealthy old customers. Veronica fit that bill perfectly.

It was about four o'clock in the afternoon when Longarm entered his rooming house and climbed the stairs to the second floor. He tried the doorknob and found it locked. That meant that Veronica was probably still out looking for a job, or else shopping for their dinner.

Longarm had a few surprises of his own. He'd stopped at his favorite liquor store and bought a bottle of French champagne for them to drink, either in celebration of her finding a job, or of coming back from Montezuma in the dangerous New Mexico Territory all in one piece.

Longarm held the champagne bottle in his left hand, and fumbled for the key to his rooms with his right hand. He found the key, inserted it into the door, and turned the lock, then the knob. The door swung open and he dropped the key into his coat pocket, then stepped inside.

He saw a battered and gagged Veronica in one

instant, and then in the very next instant, he felt a looming presence behind his half-opened door. Longarm instantly knew that there was no time to draw his gun, so he dove forward slinging the bottle up and backward even as he felt a searing sensation across his ribs.

A large, filthy man dove on Longarm with an upraised knife, and the blade missed his back and buried itself in the wooden floor. Longarm twisted under the weight of his attacker, trying desperately to get to his feet and fend off the attack. But he was at a serious disadvantage, and the knife came down just missing his neck. Longarm saw the twisted and hate-filled face of his assailant, and tried to throw up a forearm and ward off a second vicious strike.

Veronica threw herself at the man in a desperate attempt to save Custis. She rammed her head into his face and heard his nose crack like a stick. Then, arms still tied behind her back, she somehow managed to bite his broken nose as if she were a bulldog locked onto a raging bull. The man howled in pain, and Veronica felt tissue tear from his nose as blood filled her mouth. After that, she momentarily lost consciousness.

Longarm had his chance and he didn't throw it away. He rolled to his feet and kicked the man so hard in the side that his rib cage collapsed. Filled with rage, Longarm stomped the man's chest, and more ribs broke as blood poured from his nose and mouth.

"Damn you!" Longarm shouted, landing with bent knees on the man's back and then jerking back his neck until it snapped.

The man died, toes drumming against the hardwood floor.

Longarm scooped Veronica up and rushed her to his bed. He untied the gag and then her hands, noting how her wrists were chafed bloody.

"It's all right," he said over and over in his most reassuring voice. "You're going to be all right. He's dead."

Veronica opened her eyes and cried out with fright. "It's over," Longarm soothed. "I killed him. He would have gotten me instead, if you hadn't jumped into his face. You saved both our lives, Veronica."

She reached up and held him while crying. "I got the job at the dress store, Custis. And I bought us some really good champagne, but that swine drank it all. He was going to stab you to death and peel off your—"

"Shhh!" Longarm whispered. "He's not going to do anything to either of us now. He's gone."

"He was going to rape me!"

"He'll never touch another woman again," Longarm promised. "Now just take it easy. And as for your champagne, don't worry. I bought a whole magnum just for us and it's still untouched."

"You did?"

Longarm nodded. "And I'll let you drink every drop of it if you want. You saved my life today, Veronica. You deserve everything. Anything you want, I'll give you."

"Will you marry me, Custis darling? You could go to work for—"

"*Almost* anything," he amended. "Now lie still while I drag that carrion out to the fire escape and pour us some champagne before I send someone for the local police."

"Okay," she whispered.

51

"You saved my life," Longarm repeated. "And for that I'll always be in your debt."

"Can I stay here then instead of having to move out to some hotel?"

"Sure," he said. "You can stay just as long as you like."

Veronica smiled a little crookedly and wiped away her tears. "I think I love you, Custis."

"I'm afraid that could be a mistake," he said gently with his mind already focused on Montezuma, New Mexico.

Chapter 6

"All right," Billy Vail said as the train prepared to pull out of the station, "here's your first-class round-trip tickets down to Santa Fe and three hundred dollars travel money."

Longarm took the envelope and stifled a huge yawn. "I don't need to count it, do I?"

"Don't you trust me?"

"Sure," Longarm said, putting the envelope of money into the inside of his coat jacket and then handing one of the tickets to the conductor, who punched it and told him the location and number of his little sleeping compartment.

"All aboard!" the conductor shouted a few minutes later. He said to Longarm, "Better get aboard, Marshal. Glad to have you as a passenger again so soon."

"Thanks," Longarm replied, stepping up into the vestibule of the coach. He turned back to his boss on the station platform. "You look awfully worried, Billy."

"And you look exhausted. What did you do, say

good-bye over and over last night with your lady friend in bed?"

"Something like that," Longarm conceded with a lopsided grin. "When a man goes off on dangerous work, he likes to make sure he gives his lady a suitable and memorable farewell."

"Spare me," Billy said with a puritanical distaste. "Just get on the train, stay out of trouble, and get a lot of sleep. When you arrive in Montezuma and get settled, telegraph me. I'm going to have people here constantly on my back, and I have to know what you're up to or they'll badger me into an early grave."

"Billy, it might be a good idea for you to take the wife and kids up into the mountains. Go to the hot springs or to some little cabin resort where you can dip your line in a good fishing stream, lay back, and watch clouds. Life is short, Billy, and you worry way too damned much."

"And sometimes I think you worry too little."

Longarm chuckled. "Oh," he said, "on a completely different subject. You'll probably go back to the office and find time to read the local newspaper."

"I expect I will," Billy said, looking suspicious. "Why do you care?"

"Well," Longarm said as the train jolted forward. "You're going to read about a man I had to kill yesterday afternoon."

"What!" Billy shouted, trotting along the side of the train as it slowly gathered momentum.

"Self-defense!" Longarm called to his boss as the train pulled out of the station. "Don't give it two seconds of serious concern."

"Custis!"

54

"So long, Boss!"

Billy looked mad enough to chew nails when Longarm ducked into the coach. He tipped his hat to a very handsome woman in her midthirties with wavy black hair and beautiful brown eyes. "Going far, ma'am?"

"Down to Santa Fe."

"Me, too," Longarm said, noticing that she was not wearing a wedding band. "Ladies first."

She smiled with appreciation. "A gentleman, I see."

"Always," he told her with his best smile.

She nodded her pretty head and started up the aisle. And, as luck would have it, her compartment was only three down from Longarm's. Maybe, he thought with another weary yawn, he would get some shut-eye and then see if he could accidentally bump into the lady and get much better acquainted.

It was somewhere near the top of Raton Pass when Longarm and Miss Loretta Wilson finally got well enough acquainted to sneak into his compartment, lock the door, and put a whole new motion to the constant rocking of the train. Because their space was so cramped, Longarm pulled up Loretta's dress and stripped her of her undergarments before he dropped his trousers and took her standing up. Exhausted from last night's exertions with Veronica, he nonetheless had a wonderful time slamming her bare butt against the door until her knees buckled and she cried out with pleasure. Loretta bit him on the neck hard enough to draw blood, and nearly passed out when she came to a wild climax.

Moments later, when Longarm emptied his sack with a mighty thrust and a satisfying groan, they fell onto his little bunk, both laughing and trying to catch their breath.

"My heavens," she finally told him, "I didn't get a chance to see or even hold it, but it must be a *foot* long."

"Not quite," he said proudly.

"Well, it felt like it was at least that long," she told him with a kiss. "Oh, dear, your neck is bleeding!"

"Where you bit it."

She pulled back with disbelief. "I did that?"

"You sure did," Longarm said. "Good thing you didn't latch on to my earlobe or you'd have permanently disfigured me."

"I'm so, so sorry!"

"It's all right," he assured her. "I've been hurt far worse."

"You said you were a lawman. A deputy United States marshal."

"That's right."

"Have you ever been shot?"

"More times than I can remember," Longarm admitted. "But never fatally."

She smiled. "You have a cryptic sense of humor that I like."

Longarm rolled off the woman and squeezed in close beside her. "If I didn't have a sense of humor, I'd long ago have done something boring like become a farmer or harness maker. To my way of thinking, humor can be your best friend in hard times."

"I know that," she said in agreement. "I sense that you've had more than your share of heartaches."

Longarm's brow furrowed. "I wouldn't say that. I've never lost a wife or a child. To me that would be the worst kind of tragedy. But I have been in some bad fixes and seen an awful lot of blood and hard dying."

"On your job?"

"And in the War Between the States," he said quietly. "But do you mind if we change the subject?"

She shook her head. "Of course not. Are you really going to Santa Fe?"

"Almost. I'm actually getting off at Montezuma."

Her brown eyes clouded and her brow wrinkled. "I'm afraid that I know that town well. It's old and quaint, but mired in murders and mysteries."

"That's why I'm going there."

"To figure out why so many people have died lately? The mayor? The town marshal? City councilmen?"

"That's right. Loretta, can you give me any advance information? Maybe you—"

"I'm sorry, but I can't help you," she said too quickly. "I don't even want to think about Montezuma."

"Have you lived there?"

"For a while." She stared out the window at the passing landscape. "I might as well be frank, Custis. My brother was the town marshal who was stabbed to death in the Silver Spur Saloon. No one knows who did it, and I don't think anyone ever will."

Longarm digested this piece of information for several minutes before saying, "I mean to find out who killed your brother and the others. And why."

"I wish you good luck, but I'm afraid that you have no idea what you are getting yourself into."

"I'm sure that I don't. That's why I'm asking for your help in telling me ahead of time whatever you know about Montezuma and those deaths."

"I really can't help you. After my brother's funeral, I was so devastated that I had to leave New Mexico for a while or go crazy. I've been in Kansas City visiting old schoolgirl friends."

Longarm sat up. "Look, I'm sorry about your brother. I didn't mean to open up fresh wounds."

"No, that's all right. And while I am glad that you're going to try and find out who is behind the murders, I'm also concerned about your safety."

"I'm not easy to kill."

"Neither was my brother."

"I see."

She stared out through the window for a long time, and then said, "I warned my brother over and over that he should never take that job in Montezuma. He'd been a deputy in Santa Fe for less than a year when the job came open, and he desperately wanted to become a town marshal. He said Montezuma, being much smaller than Santa Fe or Taos, would be a good training ground for him, and then he'd eventually come back to Santa Fe and be qualified enough to become our town marshal. But I knew that was wrong."

"Why?"

"Homer was too nice a man to be . . ." Her hands flew to her mouth. "I'm sorry. I didn't mean to imply that *you* aren't a nice man, but I have the feeling that you are . . ."

"Harder?"

She dipped her chin. "I think you probably are. My brother was twenty-six and had never been in a gunfight. He'd just arrested drunks and troublemakers. But never had he been up against anyone or anything purely evil."

"And you think that evil is behind the murders in Montezuma?"

"Of course! And poor Homer was just too naive and trusting to believe that. He thought all the deaths were simply due to bad luck. He didn't see any connections." Tears filled her eyes. "I tried and tried to get Homer to quit that job and come to Santa Fe. But he met a girl there and that was the end of that. He just stayed until . . . until someone set him up and killed him!"

"I'll find your brother's killer and bring you whatever peace you can have from seeing the killer brought to justice," Longarm promised. "What was the girl's name?"

"Homer's girl?"

"Yes."

"Delia. Miss Delia Dawkins. She didn't even come to Homer's funeral," Loretta said with unconcealed bitterness. "I'd heard about that woman and I knew she was no good for Homer. She was just having a fling, while my poor brother thought she loved him in return. Loved him enough that they would one day be husband and wife!"

Loretta burst into fresh sobs. Longarm pulled down her dress and pulled up his pants, then comforted her as the train rolled south. He made a mental note that Miss Delia Dawkins would be one of the first people that he would go looking for in Montezuma.

Chapter 7

Longarm said good-bye to Loretta Wilson as the train approached the station at Montezuma. She kissed him tenderly and said, "Remember, you're only about thirty miles from Santa Fe. I live in an old Spanish adobe on Baca Street right near the downtown. If you run into trouble and need a friend, remember me."

"I'm sure my stay would cause at least a year's worth of gossip among your neighbors."

"Don't worry," she said with a laugh. "I live with my parents, and they will make sure that you and I sleep in separate bedrooms."

"That would kinda take the fun outa things, wouldn't it?"

"Not if we tiptoe at night," Loretta said with a wink. "Both my parents are quite elderly and hard of hearing."

"Ah! Now things are sounding better already."

"I'm serious, Custis. You have no idea of the hornet's nest that you're walking into in this sleepy-looking town."

"Montezuma!" the conductor called. "Montezuma!"

61

Longarm grabbed his bag and headed down the aisle. Out on the station platform, he waved good-bye as the train dropped off just two other passengers, then chugged south toward Santa Fe.

Longarm hoisted his bag and headed into town just as the big bell in the steeple of the Catholic church began tolling the noon hour. The weather could not have been finer, and Longarm guessed that the population of Montezuma was about equally divided between Anglos and Mexicans. Brown, white, and a scattering of Indian children played hoops and ball in the dusty streets, burros carried firewood and goods behind their owners, and the air was sweet with the scent of roses. Like nearby Santa Fe and Taos, Montezuma was an old Spanish town with a plaza. Almost all its homes were adobe with red-tile roofs. The town had an air of peaceful tranquillity that Longarm knew was deceptive.

Longarm found a nice old adobe hotel with its own private courtyard and fountain. He asked the Mexican lady at the desk to recommend good places to eat, and headed toward the plaza to find the courthouse and city hall. He found them both in less than ten minutes.

"I'd like to see the mayor," he told a man with a white handlebar mustache who was seated behind the desk reading a newspaper.

"Ain't got one no more."

"Who's the *acting* mayor?"

The man frowned with annoyance and continued to avoid Longarm's eyes while he scanned his newspaper, which was several days old. "Ain't got an acting mayor," he said, going on with his reading.

Longarm lost patience. He yanked the newspaper out

of the man's grasp and hurled it on the floor. The man jumped to his feet as if he were going to give Longarm hell or worse, but when he saw Longarm's size he sat back down again, eyes blazing with resentment.

"Don't know who the hell you think you are, mister. But I do know this, you're a pushy bastard."

"And I know this," Longarm growled back. "If you're being paid to sit behind that desk and read the news, then the taxpayers of Montezuma are getting shafted. Now, someone has to be in charge here. Tell me who he is and quit wasting my time."

"Who the hell are you to demand anything?"

Longarm took his federal marshal's badge out of his pocket and flashed it at the man without saying a word.

"Federal, huh?"

"That's right."

The man looked down at his newspaper, which Longarm was standing on with both boots. He wasn't a bit happy, but he was smart enough to know that he had better answer the question. "Mr. Douglas Ward is in charge."

"And his title?"

The man shrugged. "Headman. Top dog. Acting mayor and head of the town council."

Longarm nodded with understanding. "So where is Mr. Ward right now?"

"He's taking his lunch and then he'll take a siesta just like most of us do in Montezuma between one and three o'clock in the afternoon."

"Where's he eat lunch?"

"At Rosa's just on the other side of the plaza. But Mr. Ward don't like to talk business at lunch and he damn sure don't like to be disturbed during siesta time."

"Try to imagine how little I care what Douglas Ward likes or doesn't like," Longarm told the man as he left.

"Which one is Douglas Ward?" Longarm asked the Mexican waitress after he entered the little restaurant.

She pointed to a large, florid-faced man who was probably in his late forties and was still handsome in a beefy sort of way. Ward was seated with a couple of other men about his age, and they were all devouring tortillas and beans and washing it down with large glasses of pale beer. They were laughing and having a very pleasant meal, which Longarm figured was about to come to a sudden and serious end.

Longarm started to move toward their table, but the woman said, "Señor, if you please. Mr. Ward, he does not like to be disturbed when he eats."

"So I've heard," Longarm said with a tight smile. "Bring me a glass of beer and some food to their table."

The woman looked very worried, but Longarm didn't care. He hadn't come all the way from Denver to sit on his heels while the headman ate, drank, and then took his daily siesta.

"Mr. Ward, I understand that you are in charge of things here in Montezuma," Longarm said without preamble.

Ward was chewing on a meat-and-bean-filled tortilla. His mouth was stuffed and when Longarm addressed him, he looked up with juice streaming down his chin. To his credit, he finished his mouthful, swallowed, and then wiped his face before answering.

"That's me. Who are you?"

Longarm showed him the federal officer's badge,

and it was as if he were suddenly transformed into a very welcome and important person. Ward came to his feet and stuck out his thick, greasy hand, saying, "Welcome to Montezuma, Marshal. We have been expecting you boys."

"We aren't boys," Longarm said, taking offense at the term, "and there's just one of us and that is me."

Douglas Ward shrugged. "Well, then, welcome to you, Marshal."

"I'm Deputy Marshal Custis Long and I've come from the main office in Denver."

"Sure," Ward said, subtly trying to crush Longarm's hand, but finding that gambit impossible. "So what took you so long to come down and investigate our trouble?"

Longarm almost told him about Veronica, but he decided that would not be a good idea, so he pulled up a chair and said, "Aren't you going to introduce me to your two friends?"

"Sure," Ward said, "this is Ben Zellner and this is Ed Gill. Both are important and substantial members of our community."

The waitress brought Longarm his beer and plate of food. Longarm shook hands with the other two men, tucked his napkin into his shirt, and started eating because he was famished.

The three watched in silence for several minutes, and then Ward said, "It looks like you haven't been eating well on the way down from Denver."

"I ate well enough," Longarm replied. "But I have a strong liking for good Mexican food and this is very good."

"The best in Montezuma," Ed Gill told him. "Rosa's

has been here for generations. But you've only been here for a short time. What exactly is your business?"

"I've come to find out who murdered the former mayor and the town marshal along with the others."

"Good luck," Ben Zellner said, taking a long draw on his beer. "We've lived here most of our lives and still haven't any idea. Sure wish we did know so that we could apply some quick rope justice."

"Yeah, I'm sure," Longarm said, really enjoying his meal. "So what *do* you esteemed gentlemen know?"

"Marshal, we don't know a gawdamn thing," Ward told him. "If we did, we'd sure tell you."

"This town isn't *that* big," Longarm countered, his eyes measuring each man carefully.

Zellner and Gill didn't meet and hold his hard gaze, but Douglas Ward did, and then the man smiled. "You know, Marshal, we three are second-generation folks here. We know about all there is to know concerning Montezuma. And if we can't figure out who's behind those killings, I sure as hell don't see how you can figure it out."

"I will," Longarm vowed. "I always do sooner or later."

Ward shrugged. "How's your beer? Want another glass?"

"Not yet," Longarm replied. "You know, I always appreciate honesty and forthrightness. I have no doubt that men like you three are the pillars of this town and are looked up to by most. Be a shame if I had to dig up something that wouldn't reflect well on you. Now, wouldn't it?"

Douglas Ward's smile slipped badly. "Marshal, are

66

you suggesting that any of us had anything to do with those killings?"

"Nope. At least, I hope you didn't. But you see, when I start an investigation of a murder, I always look for *motive*. Who stands to gain and who stands to lose. Financially. Socially. Romantically. Professionally. Those are always the motives. And in this case, it seems pretty obvious to me that the stakes are high in Montezuma."

"Why do you say that?" Ed Gill demanded.

"Because you don't kill such prominent public figures as a mayor, two town councilmen, or the town marshal unless the stakes are very big."

"The town marshal's death was just the result of a drunken brawl."

"Sure," Longarm told them. "And nobody knows who put the knife in Homer Wilson's back despite it happening in a crowd. Right?"

The three shifted uncomfortably in their seats. Zellner and Gill drained their glasses of beer and jumped to their feet, saying it was time to go. Douglas Ward gave them both a hard look, then said, "Eat up, Marshal! I'll buy you another beer."

"No, thanks," Longarm said. "I've got to get to work talking to people."

"Who are you going to start with?" the acting mayor said, trying to sound real casual.

"A woman by the name of Miss Delia Dawkins," Longarm told him. "Where can I find her?"

Ward seemed to choke on his tortilla a moment before he answered. "She'll be singing tonight at the Silver Spur Saloon."

67

"I don't mean to wait until tonight," Longarm told the man. "Where is she right now?"

Douglas Ward looked like he'd just swallowed a whole chili pepper as he stammered and told Longarm where to find the woman.

"If you'll excuse us," Ward said, "we have business to attend to."

"Sure, your siestas."

Something flashed in Ward's eyes that told Longarm the man was very dangerous. "We do have other business, Marshal."

"Glad to hear that," Longarm said, not bothering to stand and shake their hands.

"How long will you be around?" Zellner asked.

"As long as it takes."

The three exchanged glances, and Longarm could see that they weren't at all happy with his answer, which gave him a very large measure of satisfaction.

Chapter 8

Longarm found Delia Dawkins at her small but neat adobe up on Baker Street. Although it was now early in the afternoon, she was still wearing a pink silk night-gown and was reading a ladies' magazine when he knocked on her door.

"Miss Dawkins?" he asked, taken aback by her manner of dress and her striking good looks.

"That's me." She waved her head and tossed her black hair. "I live here. Who are you?"

Longarm showed her his badge and said, "I'd like to have a few words with you, if you don't mind."

"Well, I *do* mind," Delia said, eyeing Longarm up and down.

"I need your help," Longarm said simply.

She stuck her head out the door and looked up and down the street. "Talking to you could get me in big trouble."

"I gotta start somewhere," he told her. "If you cared anything about Marshal Homer Wilson, I sure wish

69

you'd let me in for a few minutes. I don't know where else to begin this investigation."

She studied his craggy, earnest face and then said, "Ah, hell. You're right. You do have to start someplace. So come on in."

"Much obliged. I don't plan to stay more than a few minutes."

"Good. Because I don't want people all over town talking about us being together long enough to fool around."

He had to grin. "That's not why I'm here."

"No," she said, "I'm sure it isn't. Come on in, but wipe your feet on the mat. I'm a stickler for keeping a clean house."

"Yes, ma'am."

Longarm entered the adobe, which was cool and darker than the bright day outside. Everything was neat and tidy. The furniture was expensive, and it was clear that Delia had a flair for decorating. He removed his hat and stood looking around for a moment, and then he turned back to the beautiful woman. "Nice place you have here."

"It's no palace," Delia said, looking around with obvious satisfaction. "But it's mine, all mine. I was raised in a shanty. In winter, we froze and the wind whistled through the cracks in the wall. In the summer, we baked under a rusty tin roof. Compared to that, this abode is a castle. Now, enough of that. Would you like something to drink, Marshal?"

"Nope. I just had a big meal at Rosa's." He saw ashtrays on the end tables, and one held the butt of a little brown Mexican cigarillo. "Mind if I smoke, Miss Dawkins?"

"Certainly not. But I'll have one of whatever you're smoking."

Longarm raised his eyebrows in question, but the woman didn't seem to notice. "Thanks," she said as she took one of Longarm's cigars and then bent her head forward when he struck a match.

Delia inhaled deeply and blew out a cloud of smoke. "Not too bad," she said with a smile. "But not too good either. You're a well-dressed man, but you buy cheap cigars."

"I don't get paid that much."

"No, I don't expect that you do. Have a chair."

He thought she was extremely attractive, with reddish brown hair and a heart-shaped face. Her nightgown was cut low, and it was all that he could do to keep his eyes off the mounds of her breasts.

She followed his eyes and seemed amused. "So you've come to Montezuma to find out what happened to Homer and the others who have recently been laid to rest."

"That's right," he said, deciding to get right to the point. "Can you help me?"

"Not much. Our late mayor was an arrogant ass and nobody misses him, including his wife."

Longarm studied his cigar for a moment. "If your mayor was such an ass, how did he get elected?"

"He owned the town's only bank," Delia said. "Who's going to vote against the man that holds all the purse strings, debts, and mortgages? Our late mayor's name was Howard Trotter and he owned at least twenty percent of Montezuma. Had he lived, he probably would have managed to get his hands on half the town."

71

"Who got his share of everything after he was killed?"

"His wife, a bitch named Linda. If you want to talk to her, she's in Santa Fe, probably sleeping with half the male population."

Longarm made a mental note to see and talk to Mrs. Linda Trotter. "Obviously, you don't have a lot of love for the woman."

"No one in Montezuma liked her. She was a former prostitute, although she wouldn't admit the fact. But I met a man who screwed her in a high-class brothel in Phoenix. He was going to tell the mayor about that, but he never quite got around to it."

"Why not?"

"Well, first the mayor died, and then *he* did. He was one of the city councilmen who had a sudden accident. He now resides in our local cemetery."

"What you're saying is that Mrs. Linda Trotter had a lot to gain both by the death of her wealthy husband and by the murder of the city councilman who was going to expose her true identity."

"Yeah," Delia said. "That's *exactly* what I'm saying. If I were trying to find out who is behind all the murders in this town, I'd start out by interviewing Linda Trotter. She's a real charmer, but underneath that coat of makeup is a coldhearted bitch who would kill her own mother for money."

Longarm leaned back in the easy chair. "Just a few minutes ago I met Douglas Ward, Ben Zellner, and Ed Gill over at Rosa's. What do you have to say about them?"

"And this is a private conversation that won't be repeated?"

"You have my word on that," Longarm promised.

"Well, Marshal, I'd say that they're all somehow tied up in the murders."

Longarm's jaw dropped a little. "That's a pretty harsh statement. Any basis for it?"

Delia's eyes narrowed and she blew a circle of smoke over Longarm's head. "Doesn't it stand to reason? I mean, those three are thicker than fleas on a dying dog. The high-and-mighty Doug Ward was screwing Linda Trotter for years, and if her husband the banker wasn't such a blind fool, he'd have found out about it."

"Maybe your banker and mayor did find out about it and threatened to divorce his wife," Longarm said. "If he did that, Mrs. Trotter would have lost everything."

"I've thought of that, too," Delia said. "But the late mayor was not the kind of man to resort to threats. Besides, Doug Ward is shrewd and I'll give him that much. He'd only have married Linda if she had a bundle of money. But if she'd been thrown out by her banker husband with nothing, then Doug would have dropped her like a hot potato."

"So does Ward go to see the widow in Santa Fe?"

"I'd bet on it," Delia said. "He probably stands in line outside of Linda's bedroom along with all the other men in Santa Fe who can get a stiffy."

Longarm stifled a laugh. It was clear that Delia hated the banker's widow and would love to see her tied into the murders of her husband and the others.

"What about Zellner and Gill?" Longarm asked. "They seemed harmless enough."

"I wouldn't bet on that. They're both tough men who have proven many times that they will take what they want in Montezuma so long as Doug Ward doesn't oppose them."

"Do you see them tied together with Ward in the murder of the late banker and mayor?"

"I don't know," Delia admitted. "Both men are solid citizens of this town. However, if they didn't have anything to do with the murders, then you can bet they know who did."

"What did Marshal Homer Wilson think was going on in Montezuma?"

At the mention of his name, Delia's face hardened. "Homer saw it the same way as I did. He figured that Linda Trotter either killed her husband or had him killed and that she was up to her neck in it with Doug Ward."

"Who do you think stabbed Homer to death that night in the Silver Spur Saloon when the lights were shot out and the fight started?"

Delia's lower lip quivered. "I was working that night. I'd just gone on stage and was singing when I heard poor Homer screaming, but chairs were flying along with fists and tables, and so I ducked for cover. By the time I finally got to Homer's side, it was too late. He tried to talk, but he couldn't and died in my arms. We were in love, you know."

Longarm thought about how the lady on the train had said that Delia cared nothing for her late brother. But now watching this woman, Longarm wasn't so sure. "And so you have no idea who murdered him?"

Delia got out of her chair and began to pace back and forth in her living room, puffing furiously on the cigar. Finally, she stopped and turned to Longarm. "Marshal, you're really putting me on the spot. I've no proof. Like I said, I was in the saloon, but I didn't see it happen. If I had, I'd probably have been murdered along with the others and we wouldn't be having this private conversation."

"I understand that. But even so, I have the feeling that you know—or at least have some suspicions about—who used the knife on your town's marshal."

"I think it was either Ben Zellner or Ed Gill—and both of them were near Homer when the fight started. What I did notice was that they didn't hang around to call a doctor or help. Both of them left the instant the lights were back on in the saloon. I saw them flying out the door as if their asses had just been scalded."

Longarm nodded. "Is there anyone else here in Montezuma that was there that night when Homer died and who would talk to me?"

"Marshal Long, no one is going to tell you as much as I just have. Do you believe me?"

"Unfortunately, I do," Longarm told the woman. "And I assume you would like to see the person who stabbed Homer to death pay for it on the gallows."

"Oh, yeah, I sure would!"

"But to do that and make an arrest, I need some proof."

"You'll never get any proof."

Longarm decided to change tactics. "Delia, do you think the killings have stopped?"

The woman shrugged her bare shoulders. "I don't know. Most people think . . . or at least hope . . . that all the killing is over. But I have a feeling that maybe there is one more coming."

"Any idea who?"

"No," she admitted. "I just have a feeling that we haven't seen the end of the murders. You could call it a woman's intuition, Marshal. Any more questions today?"

"I can't think of any more right now." Longarm stood up. "Oh. Are you aware that the vice president of the United States, Chester Arthur, is coming to Santa Fe?"

Her eyes widened in surprise. "No. I had no idea. Why would he do that?"

"I don't know that, but it might be important to find out," Longarm told her. "Are there any important land or water issues going on in this part of the territory?"

Delia cocked her head a little to one side. "What do you mean?"

"I mean that out here in New Mexico—as in most of the West—land and water are what people kill for."

"Yes," she agreed, "but also for mining and grazing rights. And don't forget that Montezuma was once a boomtown flush with silver and gold ore and some big, rich mines operating."

"Have they all been worked out?"

"As far as I know, there are only a few that still operate. But I have heard rumors that there might be some new mines opening."

"Is there an assay office in Montezuma?"

"Yes. You'll find it on the same block as Rosa's. But . . ."

She didn't finish. Longarm could see that something was bothering her and he had to ask. "What's wrong?"

"The assayer is a nice man named Thad Walker. If you go there and start asking him questions, it just might put his life in danger. And remember, I said I didn't think the killings were over with. I just would hate for Thad to be the next one that gets planted in boot hill."

"I'll try to catch him where it won't be obvious to anyone."

"He has a back door to his office. If you knock on it three times, he will open the door."

"Is that your signal?" Longarm asked, knowing that it must be.

"You've asked enough questions for one day, Marshal. I hope I've been of some help."

"You have," he replied. "And don't worry about Thad Walker. I've learned how to be discreet."

"So have I," she told him with a smile. "Maybe you will want to knock on *my* back door three times one of these days."

The invitation was clear and bold. Longarm could feel the attraction between them, and she sure wasn't trying to cover up the top half of her bosom.

"Delia, you can almost count on that happening," he said with a wink while wondering how many men this woman had dangling in her web besides the late marshal and the assayer, Thad Walker.

At the door, he had a thought. "Oh, Delia. What time do you start singing at the Silver Spur?"

"Whenever the boss tells me to. Usually about nine o'clock."

"Are you any good?"

She smiled. "Honey, I'm *better* than good, but I can't sing worth shit."

Longarm couldn't help busting out in laughter as he headed down the street.

Chapter 9

Longarm knocked three times on the back door of the assayer's office after being sure that no one had watched him enter the back alley. It wasn't thirty seconds before Thad Walker threw open the door with a look of anticipation. However, when he saw Longarm instead of Delia, his expression changed to one of surprise and then disappointment.

"Who are you?"

"Deputy United States Marshal Custis Long. I need to talk to you for just a few minutes, Mr. Walker."

The assayer was tall and good-looking in a sort of intellectual or scholarly way. He was not at all the type of man that Longarm would have thought Delia would give a second glance, but you just never knew when it came to a woman's taste in men. Thad Walker wore round spectacles and his hair was moppish. He had a thin mustache and wore a suit and vest that had seen better days. His hands were slim and his fingers were stained by the chemicals that he used in his assaying work.

79

"How did you know—"

"Miss Dawkins told me to knock three times. She said that you might be able to help me."

"With what?"

"Can I come inside, please?"

Walker didn't look too pleased, but he invited Longarm into a room filled with racks of chemicals, vials, glass beakers, weights, and measures. Everything was in total disarray, yet Longarm suspected that there was a working order about the little laboratory. There was only one tall, three-legged stool, and Longarm stood while the young man took the stool, then adjusted his spectacles and fidgeted.

"I am not a neat or orderly person, unlike Delia," he admitted in his way of making an apology. "But out of this chaos there comes order. I do good and honest work here, and everyone in Montezuma knows that—and trusts me to keep my information strictly confidential."

"I understand."

"Do you?" Walker asked pointedly. "You're an officer of the law and I'm sure that you're here wanting to know about this town's murders. Well, I don't know a thing and I wish you wouldn't have come. Montezuma is a small town and there are eyes and ears everywhere. It's quite impossible to keep a secret in this town."

"So does everyone know that Delia comes in the back way and that you have a secret knock?"

Walker blushed deeply. "We didn't do that when Homer—I mean, Marshal Wilson—was alive. He was very much in love with her, you know."

"I'm sure he was. But did she love him?"

Walker swallowed hard and threw up his hands in a

gesture of resignation. "Marshal, I'm not at liberty to talk about the heart of a lady. If that's why you came, then you're wasting your time."

"I heard all about Delia and how Marshal Homer Wilson loved her even before I got off the train. That's not why I'm here," Longarm told the man. "Delia said that there are rumors about a new gold or silver strike. I have to know if that's true because, if it is, then it could be the reason why a lot of people are dying in Montezuma."

"Marshal, I . . ."

Longarm decided to stop being so pleasant. "Walker," he warned, "just answer my questions honestly and don't give me a lot of bullshit or I'll arrest you for evasion of the law."

Thad Walker blanched. The threat of being arrested wasn't real, but Longarm assumed that Thad Walker would fall for it, and he did. "Marshal, I don't want to go to jail, but I could get into serious trouble if I tell you certain things about the prospects of a new ore strike."

"Tell me anyway," Longarm said, "because I can keep your secrets. I swear to you that I will not tell any other soul what passes between the two of us in this meeting."

Walker heaved a deep sigh. "All right. There has been a new and very, very promising vein of ore discovered in this mining district. I can't say for sure, though my assay results suggest that it is worth a fortune and will impact not only Montezuma but this whole area of northern New Mexico."

"You're not exaggerating?"

"No," Walker assured him. "This discovery could be a strike bigger than the one they found on the Comstock Lode more than thirty years ago."

"That would certainly change things around here," Longarm mused. "So who owns the land where this new find has been discovered?"

"The federal government."

"What!"

"That's right. Your employer, Marshal Long. The land where the gold has been discovered is *federal land* that was once an old Spanish land grant, but later became government land when the taxes weren't paid about eighty years ago."

"How did the government get the land?"

"There was a protracted legal dispute that went on for decades, and the government finally took over the Spanish land grant for back taxes. They lease out the grazing rights to the Zellner and Gill ranching families."

Longarm frowned. "I met Ben Zellner and Ed Gill at Rosa's. So they're cattlemen, huh?"

"They are third-generation cattle ranchers. And while they own several thousand acres of deeded land, the mountain where the ore samples I've tested come from is on federal land."

"How many people know about the ore samples and their results?"

"Almost no one," Walker said. "Of course, the Zellners and the Gills know. They are the ones that brought the samples in to be assayed."

"You say this is a mountain?"

"That's right. And to make matters even more complicated, the Zuni Indians have long claimed this is their sacred mountain and have filed for it to be given to them in perpetuity."

Longarm shook his head. "Did you know that the

vice president of the United States is coming to Santa Fe?"

"Yes. I've heard the rumor."

"It's more than a rumor," Longarm said. "Do you think that all of this is perhaps somehow mixed up with that mountain?"

Walker nodded emphatically. "I'd be a fool if that hadn't occurred to me. But I just assay the ore. I don't have a thing to do with politics or ownership rights."

"Or murder."

"That's right." Walker nervously picked up a beaker and set it down again. He was clearly upset with this conversation. "Look, Marshal, what I've just told you could get me in serious trouble . . . or even worse, killed."

"I understand."

"Do you? You see, an assayer is sort of like a priest because he's sworn to secrecy about the results of his tests. If he talks, he violates a trust and once he does that, he's finished. And I don't mean just professionally if the stakes are very high."

"Relax," Longarm told the man. "Maybe this gold mountain has nothing to do with the murders, but it very well might have *everything* to do with them."

"It might."

"I assume that the Zellners and the Gills are trying everything possible to get control of that federal land."

"Yes, they are."

"And I would expect that they might even be pulling strings to get the vice president's ear on the matter."

Thad Walker nodded. "It would not surprise me in the least."

"And," Longarm continued, "I would expect that your interim mayor, Douglas Ward, has a great interest in this little secret."

"Douglas Ward is not going to be left out in the cold if there is a fortune to be made in these parts." Thad Walker started wiping off a counter. "And I won't say any more than that."

"Do you think that the late marshal knew about the new ore discovery?"

"I'm almost sure that he did. Homer Wilson was smart. He was also very ambitious."

Longarm thought about that for a moment and then said, "So you're suggesting that Marshal Wilson might have been killed because he wanted in on the discovery?"

"I'm not suggesting anything, Marshal. But then again, it's entirely possible. And here's something you should know. My assay results tell me that the ore is very high-grade. What I don't know . . . nor would anyone else . . . is how big the find is."

Walker let that sink in for a moment, then he continued. "From what Ben Zellner and Ed Gill say, it could be a huge strike. But then again, I've been in this business just long enough to know that gold is often found in pockets just as it is in veins. And sometimes . . . in fact very often . . . those pockets are just that . . . *pockets*. When that is the case, the gold is quickly worked out and there isn't any more to be found."

"So no one actually knows if it's a pocket on that mountain or a big vein of almost pure gold."

"Precisely," Thad Walker said, sounding a little excited. "But even if it is just a pocket, it will still be worth thousands."

"And if it's a large vein?"

"Millions," the assayer said without hesitation.

Longarm wanted to ask this man what he thought about the Zellner and Gill families. Did he, for example, believe them capable of murder? And what about the late marshal, mayor, and dead city councilmen? Had they also tried to somehow get in on the action?

Longarm wanted to ask, but he knew from the look on this man's face that he would not get answers to those critical questions. Thad Walker had already talked probably more than he'd intended, and he would say no more out of fear of reprisal.

"Thanks for your help," Longarm said.

"Remember, please don't tell anyone what we've discussed here. If you do, I could be killed like the others."

"I won't," Longarm promised. "But in return, I will probably be calling on you in the near future for updates."

"I really, really wish you wouldn't."

"Sorry," Longarm said, "but you have your job to do and I have mine. Besides, I'll come in from the alley again. Three knocks. Don't you and Delia change that secret signal."

Walker just looked at him.

Longarm opened the door, glanced up and down the alley to see if anyone was spying on him. "All clear. Oh, one important thing."

Walker was very nervous and impatient. He looked like he wanted to slam the door shut. "What's that, Marshal?"

"Where is the gold mountain?"

"It's called Diablo Peak. You can see it for miles around. It's about twenty miles south toward Santa Fe, and a few miles to the west."

"And exactly where were the ore samples you've tested taken?"

"I don't know," Walker confessed. "There is no reason in the world why Zellner or Gill should tell me that, and I don't even want to know."

"Yeah, I see what you mean."

"And one more thing," Walker said. "If you go to Diablo Peak, you might find the gold, but for sure you will find armed guards ordered to shoot anyone on sight."

"You're pretty sure of that?"

"Absolutely. Douglas Ward, Ben Zellner, and Ed Gill might look like ordinary city councilmen and citizens, but I'd be real careful if you plan to get involved in something that could make them all very rich."

"Oh," Longarm said, "I plan to get involved all right. I plan to get involved so much that I find and arrest murderers."

"Good luck."

"Thanks," Longarm told the man. "And if I were you, I'd be a little worried about Miss Delia Dawkins."

His handsome face clouded. "What is *that* supposed to mean?"

"Let's just say that falling in love with that woman doesn't appear to be a healthy thing to do."

Walker flushed with anger. "She had nothing to do with Homer getting killed!"

"I hope you're right," Longarm said. "It would be a real waste if such a beautiful woman spent the rest of her life in prison or ended up hanging from a noose."

Walker opened his mouth to reply, then snapped it and the door shut.

Longarm headed back to his hotel room. First thing tomorrow morning, he was going to visit Diablo Peak and he'd find where the ore samples were extracted. And when he did that, he figured he'd learn a whole lot more about these Montezuma murders.

Chapter 10

Longarm went to the Silver Spur Saloon that evening after his supper and had a few beers while watching Delia sing and dance. She had been right about having no voice, but with her low-cut dress and beautiful legs, nobody in the place cared. Hell, Delia could have croaked like a bullfrog and no one would have objected because she was such a rousing sight to the roomful of lonesome men.

At one of her breaks, she sidled over to Longarm and said, "How about a whiskey, big boy?"

"You sure you want to be seen with me?" he asked, lowering his voice. "It might not be good for business . . . or your health."

"Thad came by earlier and told me that you and he had a nice, long talk. I guess he gave you plenty to chew on, huh?"

"He did."

Her voice dropped to a whisper. "And he told you about the gold being found down at Diablo Peak."

Longarm nodded and signaled for the bartender.

"Sounds like it could change things around these parts in a big hurry."

"You got that one right. A girl like me could get rich if there is a gold strike in this part of the country. I could make a lot more money than I'm making jumping around and singing on stage."

"I saw men tossing coins and bills up there when you ended that act. You must do pretty well."

"I'm not starving," Delia admitted, "but I'm not getting rich. The other thing is that a girl has to get money while she still has her looks. You know that as well as I do."

The bartender poured their shots and Longarm started to pay the man, but Delia waved him off, saying, "It's on me, courtesy of the saloon. They don't pay me a lot, but they do pour me and my friends their best whiskey."

"Much obliged," Longarm said, raising a toast to her. "To your good health and good fortune, Delia."

"I'll drink to that," she said.

Longarm could tell that he was getting a better grade of whiskey and he smacked his lips. "Thad Walker is in love with you."

"Yeah, I know."

Longarm waited for more and when it didn't come, he said, "But I don't get the feeling that you are in love with him."

"What are you, a marriage maker or something?" She snorted, giving him a hard look. "Thad is a nice guy and we have some fun together. But he gets too serious at times and wants to get married and have a family."

"A lot of people do."

"Sure, but not people like us, huh?" Delia said with a laugh.

"You know," Longarm told her, "before he was killed, Homer Wilson had it bad for you, and now Thad feels the same way. Do you make it a habit to go around breaking men's hearts?"

The smile slipped on her face. "You're starting to get personal and I don't like that. You're here to solve murders, not love affairs or broken hearts."

"Sorry," Longarm replied, "it's just that it doesn't seem healthy for good young men to get overly attached to you."

Delia tossed her whiskey down and slammed her glass on the bar. "Marshal, this conversation is finished. Good luck with whatever you plan to do. Just stay out of my personal life and plans, okay?"

"Sure," he said, "so long as your personal life and plans have nothing to do with those murders."

Delia reared back and tried to slap Longarm's face, but he caught her wrist and the saloon fell silent. Longarm gazed into the woman's eyes and said, "Thanks for the drink and good night."

He turned and headed outside. On the corner of the street, he looked up at the moon and saw that it was full. That was good. A full moon always brought out the beast in men. And there were plenty of beasts in Montezuma, enough to go around.

Longarm slept well that night, and first thing in the morning, he had a hearty breakfast and then asked the waitress to recommend a stable where he could rent a good horse and saddle.

91

"Jake's Stable is popular and I know the owner, Jake Fernley. I can assure you that he is a fair man."

"And where can Jake's Stable be found?"

"It's just across the plaza and up the next street. There is a big sign on a red barn, so you can't miss it."

"Thanks," Longarm said, nodding to a couple of men who had stopped talking and were listening to his plans.

Longarm found Jake's Stable and then the owner, a one-legged man with a wide smile and broad shoulders. He inquired about renting a horse and was taken around the back to a corral. Following Jake, Longarm could see that the stable owner got around very well with his peg leg.

Leaning on the top corral rail, Jake said, "Take your pick, Marshal. They're all sound and well broken. How long do you want to rent the animal for and where are you taking it?"

"I'll need the horse at least three days and I'm heading south."

"To Santa Fe?"

Longarm didn't want to tell the man that he was going to see about a gold strike at Diablo Peak, so he just nodded.

"If you're only going to Santa Fe," Jake said, trying to be honest and helpful, "there's a stagecoach that leaves every afternoon at three o'clock sharp. That would save you a lot of money."

"I'd enjoy a horseback ride," Longarm said. "And I don't like stagecoaches. Crowded. Too much dust and idle talk."

"I understand," Jake told him, nodding in full agreement. "So what horse strikes your fancy?"

"I want your best animal," Longarm said. "So you tell me."

"You don't need the best if all you're doing is moseying down to old Santa Fe," Jake said. "But if you're planning on looking this country over and riding some rough trails, then I'd pick that tall blue roan with the blaze on its face and the two white stockings. He's strong and tough as boot leather. Bought him from a cowboy who got shot in the ass in a drunken fight and won't tolerate sitting in a saddle for months, if ever."

"I'll take the roan, then," Longarm said. "And I'll need tack, of course. Also, I'll be needing some supplies, so I'll return for the horse in about an hour."

"I'll have the blue grained, curried, and saddled," Jake promised. "You'll really like this gelding. He has a nice, smooth gait, or so I've been told. With only one good leg, I don't ride anymore, but I sure do miss it."

"What happened?"

"Shiloh," Jake said, his eyes clouding. "I almost lost them both and what hangs between. Cannonball hit the earth in front of me, bounced, and the next thing I knew I was on the surgeon's cutting table."

"Yeah," Longarm said, "you were luckier than most to have survived that battle."

"Were you there?"

Longarm ignored the question. "How much do I owe you for the horse and tack?"

"One dollar a day. If you bring the blue back in good condition, I'll refund you two bits a day. If he comes back lame or thin, I'll ask you for more, depending on the damage."

"That's only fair," Longarm said, heading for the

93

nearest general store to buy some supplies and ammunition. On his way he passed a gunsmith shop, and emerged a few minutes later with a good working Winchester repeater. The man had told him he would buy back the rifle at a slight discount and that suited Longarm just fine.

An hour after breakfast, he was in the saddle and trotting up the main street of Montezuma. It was still early and the street was fairly empty. Longarm looked up at the sky and thought the weather should be perfect for the ride to Diablo Peak. As he passed by the assay office, he saw Thad Walker studying him through his front window. Longarm would have given a lot to know what was on the young man's mind. Delia probably. But maybe Thad was thinking about Diablo Peak, too, and how it might just be the reason for all the recent murders.

"Hey, Marshal!"

Longarm saw Delia come out of her house with her hair mussed and her face still lined from sleep. He reined in the blue roan and leaned on his saddle horn. "Morning, Delia. I didn't expect to see you up so early."

"There's a lot about me you *think* you know, but you really don't," the woman said. "Going to Diablo Peak?"

"That's right."

"You'd better be real careful."

Longarm frowned. "Are you trying to warn me about something I should know?"

"Yes, I am," Delia said. "I heard some talk last night. Talk that was supposed to be strictly private."

"And?"

Delia folded her arms across her chest. "And I think

that you ought to stay away from Diablo Peak for a while."

"Well," Longarm told her, "I just can't do that because I have the feeling that that is where I'm going to start getting some answers instead of just more questions."

Delia looked up and down the quiet street. "Just . . . just watch yourself very carefully. I think you might be riding into an ambush."

"You *think*, or do you know?"

Delia looked up at him. "Marshal, you know as well as I do that whiskey makes loose lips and you hear a lot of brag and bullshit in a saloon. But what I managed to overhear last night sounded very serious. And that's all that I'm going to say. I've actually said enough to get my throat cut already."

"Who was doing the talking?" Longarm asked.

"Have a good, safe ride," Delia answered, heading back into her house.

Longarm touched his heels to the blue's flanks and the animal set off into an easy lope. He had twenty miles to cover before he got to that mountain where the gold was being found. And if someone was following him, he wanted to set a hard and difficult pace and pick his spots to watch his back trail.

Chapter 11

The weather was perfect and if it had not been for Delia's dire warning, Longarm would have greatly enjoyed the ride. His horse was as smooth-gaited and willing to move as promised, and Longarm pushed the animal, wanting to outdistance anyone who might be following him and planning an ambush.

He met many freighters and travelers on their way north from Santa Fe, and waved at them, but never stopped to indulge in idle conversation. For several miles, he followed a swift stream through mountains and then a low valley, enjoying the beautiful scenery.

Every three or four miles, however, he did leave the road to gain a little higher elevation so that he could see if he was being followed. And just when he was quite sure that he wasn't being followed, he saw a cluster of riders about two miles behind him riding hard.

Longarm would have liked to have a good pair of binoculars, but without them, he determined that there were four, perhaps five horsemen. He knew that they might just be cowboys heading for their home range, but from the way they were pushing their horses, Longarm thought that they had something much more urgent on their minds.

Like killing him.

So what was he to do? If he headed straight for Diablo Peak, they would find him, and perhaps even knew a few shortcuts so that they could set up an ambush.

Longarm reined in the blue roan and gave the animal a short breather while he carefully considered his alternatives. Had there been two or even three riders on his tail, he would have set up his own ambush. But with four or five . . . well, that was a little bit dicey.

"Maybe instead of going directly to Diablo Peak, I'll ride on down to Santa Fe instead," he mused out loud. "I could pay Loretta a short visit. Maybe she will know some people I should talk to about the murders and the vice president's upcoming visit."

With that decided, Longarm stayed on the road and kept pushing the roan. Loretta had told him it was about thirty miles between Montezuma and Santa Fe, but she hadn't warned him that it was a hard ride in very high and rugged country. So late that evening, he rode a weary blue roan into old Santa Fe, remembering that Loretta had told him she lived in an adobe located on Baca Street.

Longarm had no trouble finding her house and the light was on, so he tied the blue up to an apple tree and loosened the animal's cinch after giving it a few fallen apples to munch. "I'll be back to find a stable and a well-deserved bucket of grain for you," he promised, patting the sweat-streaked animal.

Longarm knocked on Loretta's door and she an-

98

swered at once. When she recognized him, she broke into a wide smile and opened her arms in greeting.

"I was hoping you'd accept my invitation to stop by for a visit," she said. "Is that your horse tied to my apple tree?"

"It is. Is there a stable close by or—"

"Never mind a stable," Loretta told him. "The Gonzalez family next door owns horses and will stable him in their barn for a very small price."

"That would be great," Longarm said, thinking that it would be wise to move the blue roan off the street and into a private barn so that he would not be found if the men who pursued him had managed to follow his trail into Santa Fe. "I'll go next door and—"

"I'll do it," Loretta said. "Custis, I'm sure you're tired from such a long ride. Go into the parlor and you'll find a crystal decanter with some very good brandy."

Longarm studied the tidy house. "On the train you told me that you lived with both your parents. I look forward to meeting them."

"I told them all about you, but of course I didn't mention the time we had in that little private sleeping compartment. They're sweet, but rather old-fashioned when it comes to the morals of their only daughter."

"I won't give them even a hint of the fun we had," Longarm promised. "So where are they?"

"They've already retired for the night. You'll meet them in the morning."

"You're assuming that I'm going to spend the night."

"Well, aren't you?" she asked, giving him a come-on smile that left no doubt Longarm would be having her undivided attention in a very short while.

"Yes," he said, accepting the enticing offer. "I would like to stay the night, but I'd rather have whiskey than brandy."

"You'll find that next to the brandy," Loretta said, giving him a kiss on the cheek and then hurrying next door to have the Gonzalez family collect and take care of his exhausted gelding.

"There," Loretta said a few minutes later when she returned. "That's taken care of. The family is very nice and they need all the extra money they can get with so many children. Don't worry about your horse or saddle; they'll be safe from thieves and well taken care of during this visit."

Longarm had already poured himself a generous whiskey and settled into what he expected was her father's favorite armchair. Now, Loretta sat down in his lap and gave him another kiss. "You'll like my parents," she said. "But you have to speak up loud or they'll just nod their heads all the while, pretending that they hear your every word."

"I'll do that," he promised.

She studied his face. "Custis, you look tired."

"I *am* tired," he admitted. "And I should tell you that I was followed out of Montezuma by four or five horsemen that probably want to kill me."

Loretta paled and didn't try to hide her alarm. "My goodness. Will they be coming here?"

"There's no reason they would know about you," he replied. "And if that blue roan is in your neighbor's backyard corral, they won't soon find me. But I'll be leaving tomorrow."

"It was wonderful of you to come and visit me so soon. Unexpected actually."

"I was hoping that you might be able to help me solve the mystery of those murders."

Her eyebrows lifted in a question. "What could I possibly do?"

"I met and talked to Miss Delia Dawkins," Longarm said. "You told me that she was a hard woman and that your brother was under her spell when he was killed in that saloon brawl."

"Yes," Loretta said. "That woman is no good . . . or did you very personally take it upon yourself to find that out?"

"No," Longarm said, realizing that Loretta was studying his face and thinking that he had probably seduced the beautiful Delia. "We talked, but that is all. She has another nice young man dangling on her string, an assayer named Thad Walker. He's in love with her."

Loretta snorted with scorn. "She's a black widow spider and this assayer you mentioned will come to ruin if he isn't careful. Delia uses men."

"She says the same thing about the late mayor's wife, Mrs. Linda Trotter. Apparently, she has moved down here to Santa Fe. I have a feeling that Mrs. Trotter might have some valuable information that could help me bust this case wide open."

"I know the woman, unfortunately. She's cut from the same cloth as Delia, only the fabric is a bit more expensive. Linda Trotter came to Santa Fe right after her banker husband was murdered."

"What is she doing now?"

101

"Lavishly spending a lot of the money she inherited from her late husband's estate."

Longarm said, "Do you think she might have had anything to do with his murder?"

"It wouldn't surprise me. Mrs. Trotter arrived here all draped in black satin as if in mourning, but that didn't last long. Very soon, she bought a fine home and was throwing expensive parties for all the politicians in Santa Fe. I think that she is either looking for a new husband, or trying to get the ear of our town's most important people."

"For what purpose?"

Loretta shrugged. "I'm not quite sure."

Longarm sipped his whiskey. "I'd like to find her and ask her some questions tomorrow morning. Do you know where the woman lives?"

"Of course. She bought an imposing Victorian house, white with yellow trim, located on Agua Fria Street overlooking our Santa Fe River. It's one of our oldest and nicest homes and situated among the wealthiest and most influential people in town, of course."

"Of course." Longarm stood up. "I've been told that Mrs. Trotter is very well acquainted with Montezuma's new acting mayor, Douglas Ward."

"So I've heard. But—"

"Don't you see how this all ties together?" Longarm said.

"I'm afraid I don't."

Longarm smiled. "It's like this. Mrs. Trotter inherits a fortune, and now I'm told the new mayor of Montezuma is about to grab ownership of a mountain of gold. Once they accomplish those aims, they could just

102

about do anything they wanted in northern New Mexico. They would be a force to be reckoned with in this part of the country."

"So you think that's it?"

"I do," Longarm told her. "I believe that everything revolves around the discovery of gold. It's at Diablo Peak. But I've learned that there is one major complication."

"And that is?"

"Diablo Peak is on government—not private—land."

Loretta nodded as comprehension set in. "So that might be why they are trying so hard to get the visiting vice president's ear. He would probably have the power and influence to change Diablo Peak from public to private ownership."

"And," Longarm added, "also take care of the Zuni problem."

"Zuni?"

"Yes," Longarm said. "I've learned that the Zuni are claiming Diablo Peak to be their ancient and sacred mountain."

Loretta poured herself a drink. "It's all very complicated, isn't it?"

"Afraid so," Longarm agreed, "and the stakes are very, very high. I've met Douglas Ward. He's smooth, articulate, and ruthlessly ambitious. He has two powerful friends and prominent ranchers on the city council named Zellner and Gill. What I think is that all of them are in cahoots to get Diablo Peak's gold and then to have Ward become the governor of this territory, and perhaps even move into national politics."

"Douglas Ward is *that* ambitious?"

"Yes," Longarm said, "I'm sure of it. His ambition may be matched only by the ambition of his secret ally, the widow Linda Trotter, who you say is now wining and dining all the most important people of Santa Fe."

"And my brother? How did Homer come to be murdered in the Silver Spur Saloon?"

"I'd like to think that he knew about the conspiracy to grab Diablo Peak and threatened to expose the participants. For that he was killed."

"Or perhaps my brother wanted a piece of the pie and they weren't willing to give it to him."

"I'd rather think that he acted honestly," Longarm said, "and I'm sure you would, too."

"Yes," Loretta said quietly. "Homer was a good man and honest when he became town marshal. I choose to think that he also died an honest public servant."

"Me, too," Longarm said.

"So what you've laid out here makes perfectly good sense," Loretta said. "But how long are we going to have to talk?"

"What do you mean?"

Loretta took away his glass of whiskey and started unbuttoning Longarm's shirt. "It's getting late and I'm a working woman, remember? I have a class waiting to be taught at the schoolhouse tomorrow morning, and I do need at least some sleep."

Longarm let her unbutton his shirt. She began to kiss his chest and then to fumble with the buttons on his pants.

"Where is your downstairs bedroom?" he asked.

"Right this way, Marshal."

Longarm took Loretta into her bedroom and closed

the door. Moments later, he and the Santa Fe school-teacher were wildly making love. Longarm was tired from a long day in the saddle, but getting into Loretta's soft saddle was an entirely different and far more pleasurable experience.

"Oh, Custis," she moaned as he thrust harder and harder into her soft honey pot. "Don't stop. Please don't ever stop!"

"I have to because you need some sleep and so do I," he groaned as he reached under her, grabbed her heaving buttocks, and then filled her with his hot seed until they both lay spent and quivering.

A short time later, Loretta snuggled up close to him and whispered in a soft and sleepy voice, "Don't you dare screw the Widow Trotter tomorrow morning. Or that damned Delia back in Montezuma, for that matter."

"I'll try to remember that," he said, only slightly awake.

"And be careful when you talk to Mrs. Trotter. There is so much at stake here that she would poison you with a morning cup of coffee, if that was what she thought it took to achieve her ambitions."

"I'll ask for tea," he said with a yawn.

"Better yet, Custis, don't drink or eat *anything* with Mrs. Trotter."

"Okay," he said, falling asleep with Loretta in his arms.

Chapter 12

The next morning before Loretta's parents awoke, Longarm left the adobe on Baca Street and went to see Linda Trotter in her big Victorian home by the Santa Fe River. It wasn't a long walk, so he didn't bother collecting his horse, but instead left it for a few more hours of rest and feeding in the Gonzalez family's backyard corral.

Longarm stopped for a hearty breakfast of steak and eggs in the downtown area, and had a few cups of strong coffee between yawns. He and Loretta had awoken and made love together several times during the previous night, and Longarm was still a little sleepy. That wasn't good because he would need to be sharp when he met and confronted the widow woman in a short while.

It was half past nine o'clock when Longarm knocked on the door of the tall and stately Victorian, which he thought probably cost a fortune. The newly widowed Mrs. Trotter answered the door looking a little hungover, perhaps from a late-night party.

"Yes?" she said through the crack in her door.

Longarm showed the woman his badge and asked if he might step inside and ask a few questions about the murder of her husband, the late Montezuma banker and town mayor.

Linda Trotter was tall and slender, with long auburn-colored hair combed back straight from her rather high forehead. In her early thirties, she was not a beautiful woman with her slightly protruding upper teeth and a nose that was a bit too large for her long face. And yet, the widow had a certain elegance and sharp intelligence about her that was unmistakable.

"Marshal Long, my husband, Howard, has been dead for much longer than a month," she said. "I'm no longer in mourning and I'm trying to get on with a new life here in Santa Fe. So I'm really not too pleased to bring up the subject anymore."

"It will only take a few minutes of your time, Mrs. Trotter. And I've heard that you are making many friends here in Santa Fe along with making a very favorable impression."

"That remains to be seen," she said, opening the door and letting him inside before taking his hat and hanging it on a hat tree. "I hope that you have some important news concerning my late husband. Otherwise, I will ask you to please leave, as the subject of Howard's untimely death is still quite upsetting to me."

"I'm sure that it is," Longarm said in his most solicitous manner. "And I promise you that I will be brief."

"Good. Please come into the parlor and have a seat." She led off and he followed, noticing that she had a nice set of hips and that they swayed as she walked. "Marshal, would you like some tea or perhaps coffee?"

108

Remembering Loretta's warning last night as they lay in her bed, Longarm declined. "No, thanks."

"So," she said, taking a seat in the parlor. "Tell me why you have come here to see me in Santa Fe."

Longarm had anticipated the question. Unfortunately, he still didn't have a very good reply that might get the woman to reveal any of her secrets, so he blurted out, "I understand that your husband and the new mayor of Montezuma, Douglas Ward, were close friends and business associates."

"*Close* friends?" She frowned and pretended to give the matter a good deal of consideration. "Marshal Long, to be frank, I would never say they were close friends. But I suppose that they did do some business things together. Douglas Ward was a city councilman and had a good deal of influence in Montezuma. He was also a very nice gentleman, but I don't think my late husband and Douglas really had much in common."

Longarm decided to lob a cannonball at her and see if he could shake her steely outer defenses. "Other than *you*, Mrs. Trotter. Other than you."

She paled and jumped to her feet, clearly shaken to the core. "What on earth are you suggesting by that uncalled-for remark!"

Longarm had put his foot into it too deep and there was no backing down now, so he took a gamble and replied, "Just that I know that you and Douglas Ward are lovers and have some grand ambitions centered on getting ownership of Diablo Peak and the fortune in gold that it probably holds."

Her eyes widened and she cried, "What!"

Longarm had to give the woman credit because,

although she was shocked to the very marrow of her bones, she made a remarkably fast recovery. "Marshal, you are totally mad! What . . . or who . . . on earth has fed you such horrible lies!"

"Several people that are honest and trustworthy."

She paled with anger and also a measure of well-deserved fear. "I think you should leave right now! In fact, I *demand* that you leave this very moment!"

Longarm came to his feet. "I suppose I should say that I am sorry to have upset you. However, I'm not. And if I hadn't spoken the truth just now, then you would never have gotten so rattled and upset."

"Out of my house!" she cried, fists balled and shaking.

Longarm wanted to give her one last parting shot to send her to the very abyss of fear. "Mrs. Trotter, before I go, allow me to make you a promise. I know that you were part of a conspiracy to have your late husband murdered, along with others in Montezuma. I guarantee that your scheme with Douglas Ward will fail."

She was nearly in tears. "Leave this house!"

Longarm started for the hallway. He retrieved his hat and placed it on his head. "Furthermore, Mrs. Trotter, I believe that you are a liar and murderess. And I am quite sure that you, Douglas Ward, Ben Zellner, and Ed Gill are the ones behind all the Montezuma murders."

"You are insane!"

"No, I'm not." Longarm put his hand on the doorknob. "Oh, and one more thing. I will make it my personal mission not only to get proof about your involvement, but also to make sure that Diablo Peak and whatever gold it may possess never falls into your greedy and bloody hands."

Longarm thought that Linda Trotter was going to attack him. If she'd had a gun, he was sure that she would have shot him dead in the entryway to her beautiful Victorian home. But luckily, she was unarmed as he smiled and closed the door behind him.

"Well, Custis," he said to himself as he walked briskly down the street overlooking the scenic Santa Fe River, "you have really set things in motion. Now, it's absolutely assured that you are a marked man."

Longarm returned to Baca Street, chatted with Loretta's sweet and elderly parents for a few minutes, shouting the entire time so that they really heard him, and then he gathered his belongings and penned a quick note.

My dear Loretta

I visited the widow in supposed mourning and decided to rattle her cage and see what fell out. I told her that I knew she and Douglas Ward were party to the murders of your brother and the others in Montezuma. As you would expect, Mrs. Trotter went nearly crazy with anger and threw me out. Now, I'm sure that she will be getting in contact with all those involved in the murders and they will come at me with a vengeance.

It seemed the only way to set things in motion, and I need to distance myself from you and your dear parents so that you are not also in extreme danger. Please do not try to contact me. I will survive and the guilty will be caught and punished very soon.

Sincerely, Custis Long

Longarm left the note where Loretta would be sure to discover it when she was finished with teaching for the day and returned home. Then, he went next door and paid the Gonzalez family twice the agreed-upon fee for boarding his horse in their backyard.

"Vaya con Dios!" Mr. Gonzales called as Longarm mounted up, admiring how nice his horse looked from a vigorous currying and plenty of oats.

"Gracias, Señor Gonzalez!" he shouted as he put the blue roan into a trot and headed for a showdown at Diablo Peak.

Chapter 13

Longarm was quite sure that he would not be followed out of Santa Fe. The men who had followed him down from Montezuma were either waiting in ambush at Diablo Peak, or they had gone into Santa Fe in the hopes of finding and killing him there.

As he rode north and then cut west into higher mountains, he kept his eyes peeled for Diablo Peak, described as looking like Pikes Peak in Colorado, only much smaller. And sure enough, by noon he could see the peak jutting up into the clear New Mexico sky.

Longarm rode straight for the peak, but when he got to within about two miles of Diablo, he tied the blue roan in among some big rocks where it could not be seen. Taking his Winchester rifle and plenty of ammunition along with a canteen of water, Longarm decided to hike in close, where he was almost certain to find heavily armed guards and miners.

It took him about an hour to move in close to the peak, and then nearly as long to sneak around Diablo until he saw signs of activity. Crouched behind some pines, he saw several ore wagons, canvas tents, and smoke drifting off a campfire. There were at least four miners extracting ore from a mine tunnel located about halfway up the side of the peak. Near the tunnel were two more small caves, one of which was partially covered up and hidden by carefully placed rocks, sticks, and gravel.

Longarm took a drink of water and settled down to wait and see what developed. He thought he recognized some of the men working on the side of Diablo Peak, but the only one that he could identify for certain was Ben Zellner. Zellner was clearly in charge and was overseeing the work.

Longarm hunkered down and waited for the cover of darkness. He wasn't sure what his next move would be, other than he could arrest all of these men for stealing gold off government land without ownership or a mining permit. Also, he wanted to see where the ore was being taken, and he suspected it would be to either Zellner's or Gill's private ranch property. If they dumped it on either of those men's property, it could later be claimed that the ore belonged to the pair of ranchers.

Late in the afternoon, one of the wagons, now loaded with ore, left Diablo Peak. It was a heavy load and pulled by a team of ten strong Missouri mules. Longarm decided to follow the wagon, so he went back and got his horse. By early evening, he had passed onto the Zellner ranch, and soon he saw that he had been correct and that the gold-bearing ore was being laboriously unloaded by shovels and added to a huge cache. "They're stealing from government property," he said aloud to himself.

Longarm decided to ride back to Diablo Peak and camp out for the night. By first light he would be hiding up in the tunnel, and then he'd spring out and arrest the miners and guards. He had counted just two armed guards and the miners, and knew the miners would give him no resistance.

It was a long, cold night because Longarm hadn't thought to bring a sleeping roll and so he'd had to bundle up in his coat and horse blankets without a warming campfire. He was stiff and tired when he began to hike up to Diablo Peak in the predawn darkness. Fortunately, the moon was full and high, so he did not stumble around in the loose rocks that ringed the rugged and almost treeless peak. Longarm crept past the ore wagons, and then moved soundlessly around the sleeping camp. Being as absolutely quiet as possible, he hiked up the side of Diablo Peak until he reached the tunnel where all the rich gold ore was being extracted.

Longarm ducked inside the tunnel and hunkered down to wait. In less than a half hour, he knew that the sun would come up in the east and that the camp below would come to life.

His timing was just right. Only a few minutes after entering the mine tunnel, Longarm observed someone get up in the semidarkness and start the campfire. A short time later, the silhouetted man placed a pot of coffee over the fire to boil. Soon, other men were waking up as the sun lifted sluggishly over the distant mountains. The camp was about fifty yards below the mining tunnel, and the men got dressed and set about cooking pork and sourdough flapjacks. The aroma of

115

their cooking food made Longarm realize that he had not eaten since yesterday at noon. Maybe, he decided, I'll have some of their breakfast after I've got them tied up good and tight.

By seven A.M., according to Longarm's pocket watch, the men finished their food, last cup of coffee, and morning smoke, then gathered up their picks and shovels. As they started up the steep peak toward the tunnel where Longarm waited, he could hear them talking.

"Hands up!" he shouted as they started to enter the tunnel where he was waiting.

The miners dropped their tools and threw up their hands. The lone guard, however, threw up his rifle and tried to fire. Longarm shot the man in the chest, and then turned his gun on the surprised hard-rock miners, saying, "Unless you boys want to end up as dead as that fool, do as I say!"

The miners raised their hands. A big fellow with a thick, bushy beard said, "Who the hell are you?"

"I ask the questions," Longarm replied. "Are any of you packing a gun or knife?"

The miners shook their heads, indicating that they were unarmed. Longarm said, "Keep your hands up in the air and walk single file back down to your camp. If anyone tries to escape, I'll shoot him down just like I did the guard."

"You gonna steal some gold ore and then kill us?" the same big miner demanded.

"Nope." Longarm showed them his badge. "I'm a federal officer and you are digging gold on *public* property."

"Mr. Zellner said this peak was on his ranch!"

"Well," Longarm answered, "Zellner lied and he's

116

going to prison for it. If you do as I say, you men might get off with jail time."

"We didn't know this was government land. Mr. Zellner said—"

"I don't care what Zellner, Gill, or anyone told you," Longarm said, cutting the man off in midsentence. "You're all under arrest for mining on public land. Now move on down to your camp!"

The big one growled, "Mr. Zellner and Mr. Gill aren't gonna like this, Marshal. You're stepping into a whole lot more trouble than you know."

"I'll worry about them and you worry about me," Longarm warned. "Now let's go!"

He marched the miners down the side of the peak and into the camp. "Any coffee or breakfast left over?"

"Hell, no!"

They were all glaring at him, wanting to fight. Longarm saw some rope. He ordered the miners to lie down, faces to the ground, and put their hands behind their backs. When the big one objected, Longarm put a bullet about an inch past his head, and the miner had a sudden change of heart.

Longarm got them all tied at the wrists and ankles.

"What are you gonna do with us now?" one of the prisoners asked.

"I'm thinking on it," Longarm admitted.

"You mean you got us all tied up like this and you don't even know what you're going to do with us?" the big man bellowed with indignation.

"Yep," Longarm said, "that's the way it is right now. When are the ore wagons that left last night due back from Zellner's ranch?"

They fell into a sullen silence.

Longarm cocked back the hammer of his gun and said, "Who wants to die this morning?"

"They'll be back by noon, dammit!"

Longarm uncocked the hammer and asked, "How many men?"

"How should we know!" the miner shouted in anger. "We're just doin' honest work for honest wages."

"I have my doubts about that. But we'll just let that pass until after I've cooked some breakfast and made another pot of coffee."

"You're going to *eat* while we lie here hog-tied?" the big miner roared in a fury. "Gawdammit, Marshal! That ain't right!"

"Sure it is," Longarm said almost cheerfully. "You boys had a good night's sleep, then you enjoyed a fine, big breakfast, but I got neither. Now, I'm making up for it."

Longarm sliced some pork and located the fixings to make more sourdough flapjacks. The coffeepot was still a quarter full, so he poured himself a steaming cup and smacked his lips with satisfaction. "Strong and black! Just the way I like it."

He had a big breakfast while the hog-tied miners growled and grumbled with increasing discomfort. He understood that they were worried and physically uncomfortable, but they would survive. He really had no quarrel with these hardworking men, and he'd decided to release them as soon as he felt they could not cause him any injury or trouble.

Longarm finished his second plate of pork and flapjacks and his third cup of coffee. He felt much better now and not nearly as sleepy.

"Why don't you just let us go?" the big miner asked, not bothering to hide his bitterness. "We'll just hitch up that little buckboard with a couple of mules and all be on our way with no hard feelings toward you."

"You'd drive straight to the Zellner ranch, I'll bet," Longarm replied. "And you'd sound the alarm and then I'd have a whole bunch of armed-to-the-teeth gunnies headed this way as fast as they could ride. No, thanks."

"Then we'll go down to Santa Fe instead," the man said, his voice getting desperate. "That's where we were hired. Some of us have families there. We didn't sign up for trouble, Marshal. We just wanted to feed our families and make a livin'."

"That's probably true," Longarm admitted. "But didn't it arouse even a little bit of suspicion when the ore you took out of that tunnel was hauled over to the Zellner ranch and just dumped in an empty wash? I mean, why would anyone go to all the trouble of loading that ore and then simply dumping it in a wash out in the middle of nowhere?"

His question caused some of the miners to squirm, and Longarm was sure that they had known that Diablo Peak rested on public land and that what they were doing was illegal.

"No answer, huh?" Longarm said, looking at each of the bound miners. "Well, I didn't really expect one. But I might just let you men get off with just a little jail time in Santa Fe."

"You would?"

"Sure," Longarm said with a smile. "Because I'm really after the big fish. That would include Montezuma's new acting mayor, Doug Ward, along with the councilmen and ranchers Ben Zellner and Ed Gill. They're the ones that are going to prison. You boys wouldn't have to do more than a month in jail."

"A month!" an Irishman cried.

"Shut up, Riley!" their leader warned.

"I can't spend a month in a stinkin' jail," Riley protested. "I got three hungry mouths to feed."

Longarm didn't even try to look sympathetic. "You know," he drawled, "I do understand and I might even let you men go this morning, if you told me what you know about Ward, Zellner, and Gill."

"They've *all* been here," the Irishman said hopefully.

"Riley, you've been warned to shut your damned trap!"

"Well, all three have been here!" Riley stubbornly persisted. "And they told us this was private land and that we'd get a fine bonus if this ore assayed real high. Now, I'm lyin' here hog-tied and feelin' low and this marshal is tellin' me that we might all have to do a month of jail time!"

The big miner and the Irishman began a heated argument, and Longarm let them go at it for a while. He expected that Riley or even one of the other miners would break and tell him enough to arrest the leaders of this deadly mining scheme.

"Boys, boys!" Longarm finally said as he smoked a cigar. "What I really want to know is who is behind all the killing that has gone on at Montezuma. Now, I know that it's all because of this gold ore. But I could use some witnesses."

"No bloody way!" the big miner shouted. "Riley, I'll cut your damned throat if you say another word!"

Longarm had an idea. He went over to the Irishman named Riley, who seemed more inclined to cooperate, and cut the man's bindings. Then he jerked the miner to his feet, pushed him off to the side, and said in a low voice, "You want to tell me what you know about those killings?"

"Why should I do that?"

"Because," Longarm explained, "if you do, then not only will I let you loose, but I'll give you twenty dollars."

He slipped a gold piece out of his vest pocket and then slipped it into Riley's pocket without the others noticing the exchange.

"Little good your money will do me or my family if I'm lying in a grave," Riley hissed, daring to glance over his shoulder at the others.

"Tell me what you know right now in private and then we can pretend that you said nothing, and that way you won't have to worry about those men killing you."

"We could do that?"

"Sure," Longarm whispered. "Tell me what you're hiding."

Riley looked scared half to death, and his head kept swiveling back toward the others, who were still hog-tied and glaring at him with blood in their eyes. Long-arm didn't think that Riley was going to help, but then the Irishman hissed in a low voice, "Marshal, do you swear that you'll protect me and my family?"

"I swear it," Longarm said. "You get to keep that twenty-dollar gold piece and I'd never break our promise."

"Well," Riley whispered, "I don't know for dead certain, but I think that you need to dig out those other two closed tunnels. Might be that you'd find they were really. . ."

Riley's voice failed because he was filled with so much fear.

"What's in those two closed tunnels!" Longarm pressed. "Come on and tell me!"

"You'd find . . . *graves*," Riley said, his voice quietly cracking.

Longarm didn't look at the closed-up tunnels located not far from the working mine tunnel. But now he knew that sooner or later he'd have to inspect them.

"Thanks, Riley. I'll see that no charges will be filed against you. Now we have to make a show so that your friends also believe that you wouldn't help me."

"How—"

Without answering, Longarm drove his fist into Riley's gut . . . hard. The Irishman doubled over and collapsed gagging on his knees. Longarm stood over him and shouted, "Damn you, Riley! Tell me what I want to know or I'll beat your stupid brains out!"

Riley shook his head, and Longarm hit him again. It looked like a powerful chopping punch with power, but it really wasn't. The blow Longarm delivered was just hard enough to send Riley sprawling in the dirt with bloody lips. And while the other miners watched in horror, Longarm reared back and pretended to deliver a vicious kick to Riley's side.

Riley, now on to Longarm's ruse, screamed as if he were dying.

Longarm, snarling, grabbed the Irishman and dragged him over to the others. "I thought your friend Riley had good sense, but he doesn't have any at all. He should

122

have cooperated, and now I'm going to take each one of you men and give you what I gave Riley if you don't tell me what I want to know!"

They stared at the bloodied and seemingly dying Riley and were terrified. One of the miners had started to tell Longarm everything he already knew when, suddenly, a rifle shot whip-cracked across the distance.

Longarm felt a bullet crease his shoulder and he spun around. More rifle shots came in rapid succession, and Longarm didn't have time to get his Winchester.

"Shoot him!" several of the miners screamed at the riflemen who were charging up the side of Diablo Peak. "He's a United States marshal!"

The bullets were coming fast and furious, and Longarm knew that there was only one place close by where he might survive just a little longer. So without an instant's hesitation, he wildly scrambled up the peak and dove headlong into the open mining tunnel with bullets chasing him like a swarm of hornets.

Chapter 14

Longarm threw himself on the rocky floor just inside the mouth of the cave. He drew his Colt and slowly raised his head to take aim on the first stupid sonofabitch who thought he could charge up the side of Diablo Peak and burst into the mining tunnel.

He didn't have long to wait. A man with a Winchester and a red beard appeared, and Longarm stayed flat on the ground in the darkness of the tunnel until the fool was nearly on top of him. Then, with a cool and deliberate aim, he shot upward into the man's guts, and then shot him again under the jaw just for good measure. The rifleman crashed just a few feet away from Longarm, dead before he struck the floor. Longarm grabbed the fool's rifle and sidearm.

"Some men are too brave for their own good, but I think you were just stupid," Longarm told the twitching corpse as he took aim on another man who also seemed interested in committing suicide. Levering a shell into the Winchester, Longarm fired, but his bullet went a little to the left, hitting the man in the forearm and no doubt shattering it badly. The man screamed, reversed direction, and dove into some brush, howling in agony.

"What we have here is a standoff," Longarm said, making a mental note that this hard-used Winchester rifle shot wide left.

The men down below were furious. They distributed weapons to the miners, and everyone began firing up at the mouth of the tunnel, creating a thunderous volley. Longarm realized that they were hoping a ricochet would hit and kill or at least badly wound him.

Then someone shouted, "Hold it! Hold your fire! There's dynamite up in that tunnel!"

"Good!" another man cried. "If we hit it, the dynamite will blow that big sonofabitch to hell!"

"Yeah and the tunnel will be destroyed and that would take weeks to clear out!"

Longarm felt a shiver of fear run up and down his spine, and he glanced over his shoulder toward the back of the tunnel. "Dynamite!" he said aloud.

He pressed closer to the floor and listened to his heart begin to race. He wasn't ready to make this tunnel his grave, but he didn't seem to have a whole lot of choice regarding the matter.

"Marshal!" a man bellowed. "You can't get out of that tunnel so you might as well surrender."

"Like hell I will," Longarm shouted back, already deciding that he would wait until it was dark and try to make his escape. Then he remembered that the moon was nearly full and at night he would be very visible to the riflemen below.

"Damn," he swore to himself.

"If you come out," the man called, "maybe we can make you a deal!"

Longarm barked a defiant laugh. "I'd rather make a deal with the devil!"

Someone fired an angry shot, and that caused a lot of new shouting down below. It seemed they wanted him dead, but they sure didn't want the tunnel to be destroyed.

"Marshal, we can be reasonable. It's all just a matter of how much money you need."

"Is that you, Ward?"

"No. I'm Ben Zellner. Ed Gill is also with me. We're not looking to kill a federal marshal. We can work this out like reasonable men."

Longarm had to chuckle. This type always thought that everyone and everything was for sale. "Let me think on it!" Longarm called out, playing for more time.

He examined where a bullet had creased his shoulder. The wound was bleeding, but it wasn't deep or life-threatening. Longarm put the pain aside and edged back into the cave to see what he could find that might be useful.

The tunnel ran back about thirty feet, and at the rear wall he found a fifty-gallon water barrel that was nearly full. A bullet had pierced the barrel, but fortunately very near the lid, so not much water was lost. Longarm took a couple of swallows and then looked around for something else of value. Unfortunately, there was no food. However, he knew that a man could go for days without food, but not nearly so long without water, and he knew he'd gotten lucky. He also found a box of dynamite with just four sticks left in the box. All the rest had apparently already been used in blasting this tunnel. There were also some picks and shovels, which he didn't think would serve him any good purpose. And three or four kerosene lamps. The tunnel itself had been shored up with timbers and the lamps were hanging on nails.

Other than those items, Longarm could see nothing more of value.

He started to creep back toward the mouth of the tunnel, then stopped and returned to the wooden box holding the four sticks of dynamite. Longarm realized that they might be his ticket out of this tunnel, so he stuffed them all into his coat pockets. He had matches and a good throwing arm. If worse came to worst, he would go out slinging explosives.

The dynamite and the water gave him plenty of fresh hope as he returned to the entrance of the tunnel and dragged the man he'd just killed deeper inside. Longarm went through the dead man's pockets, finding nothing he could use. Just a cheap folding knife, a brass pocket watch, and less than a dollar in coins.

"You were not only stupid, but you were damned poor," Longarm said to the body whose blood was seeping into the floor.

Longarm placed the man's pistol and Winchester near the mouth of the tunnel and hunkered down for a rest. He would have to be careful not to fall asleep, although he didn't think that the men below were going to risk a frontal attack, given that one of them had already had his last ticket punched and another had had his arm shattered.

Longarm realized he'd dozed off. When a voice roused him, he saw that the sun was getting low on the western horizon.

"Marshal!"

"What!"

"We're getting tired of waiting!"

"Well," Longarm called, "you're going to get a lot more tired because I'm not going anywhere soon!"

"Dammit, we can outlast you!"

"I'm sure you can," Longarm replied, "but there's plenty of water up here and someone was kind enough to leave a chunk of jerky, so I'm doing just fine."

Longarm heard the men below arguing, and he supposed Gill or Zellner was trying to determine if there really was water and jerky up in the mine. Maybe they'd figure out there was no jerky, but they'd be furious when they learned about the nearly full water barrel.

Finally, Zellner shouted, "There's no one coming to help you, Marshal! No one at all. We can wait here for *days. Weeks,* if that's what it takes. You'll eventually run out of food and water. You'll get weak and then it will all be over!"

"Nobody lives forever," Longarm called down to Zellner. "And by the time I'm dead, there will be other federal lawmen here to investigate. I know *everything*, Zellner. I know that you, Ward, and Gill are behind all the Montezuma murders."

"You can't prove that! You're just blowin' smoke out your ass!" Ed Gill screamed.

"Am I?" Longarm yelled down to them. "We'll see!"

"Let's open fire and to hell with blowing up the tunnel!" Zellner swore, unleashing three wild bullets that ricocheted down the length of the tunnel.

Longarm was glad that he had the four sticks of dynamite in his pocket and that his pocket was pressed close to the rock floor. Given where he was lying, there seemed no way that a stray bullet could ricochet off the walls and strike either him or the dynamite.

"We're going to have a nice supper, Marshal. Steaks and some whiskey to wash it down. Too bad you can't be reasonable and come to your senses. If you did, we would all be better off. You could eat with us and have some whiskey and—"

"And get my throat cut in the night!" Longarm yelled. "Do you really think I'd trust a band of murderers?"

Zellner was rabid. "We'll take you alive! And when we do, we'll skin you like a jackrabbit, you sonofabitch!"

"Big talk!" Longarm shouted. "What are you waiting for? Come and get me!"

Overcome with helpless rage, Zellner fired up at the tunnel until his Colt revolver was empty. Then Longarm heard the man curse in fury and frustration.

Longarm laughed, and the sound of it echoed down Diablo Peak and into the canyons and valleys.

It was dark, but the moon was almost full. Longarm could not see any men, but he could see the sparks from their large campfire. He heard some laughter, and he figured that they were drinking whiskey. Maybe they were drinking it in order to work up the courage to attack him. If so, Longarm figured he could kill five or six of them before they could get up to his mine tunnel. And to tell the truth, he didn't think they could muster up enough whiskey courage to be *that* drunk and crazy.

So what was he to do about his predicament? Longarm lit a cigar and leaned his back against the rocky side of the tunnel. He idly wondered if he might be surrounded by a vein of pure gold, but it was too dark to tell. Not that it mattered. There was gold in this tunnel, or else the men below would simply ride away except for maybe one or two who would try and outwait him.

Longarm knew that time was not on his side. He'd been bluffing about the jerky, of course. And as the days slowly passed, he would weaken and be less able to repel an attack. The only thing that was keeping the men below off him now was the fact that he had the advantage of being uphill. If they charged this tunnel, they would have to scale the side of the peak and it would be slow, bloody work.

However, even with the advantage of his elevation, Longarm decided that it was pointless to wait. His best odds would be to light the dynamite and then charge out of the tunnel and take his chances even in this semi-darkness.

"All right," he said, extracting the four sticks of dynamite from his coat pocket. He braided their fuses together so that he could light them all with one match, and then he took a deep breath. "This better work!"

On second thought, he untangled the fuse of one stick and put that one back in his coat pocket. Three sticks of dynamite thrown as he burst out of this tunnel would do almost as much good as four. And the fourth might just come in handy in the desperate minutes after he left the tunnel. Longarm was counting on the fact that his blue roan was still hidden only a mile or so distant. And he would need to get to that animal to have any chance of survival.

He took a deep breath, stuffed the dead man's pistol

into his waistband, and grabbed up the Winchester that shot wide to the left.

"Here goes!"

Longarm snapped a match on his thumbnail and touched it to the three fuses braided together. They flared and hissed. It took all of his nerve not to immediately pitch them down toward the campfire as if they were burning his palms. But he waited and stared at the fuses as they burned and burned. Finally, when he judged that they had about five seconds left before explosion, Longarm jumped out of the tunnel and heaved the bundle with all of his strength.

Someone must have seen the sparkling package of death lobbed at them through the air because just before the explosion, Longarm heard a high-pitched shriek of terror.

The explosion sounded like the collision of two runaway freight trains. The blast rocked Diablo Peak, and even though Longarm knew that he could not possibly have thrown the sticks far enough to land directly into his enemy's camp, they landed close enough to kill or stun every man below.

Rocks and flames shot into the moonlit sky. A horse's scream rose up in the cloud of death. Smoke and fire seemed to envelop a hundred-foot radius and light the peak for an instant like the sun.

Longarm snatched up the rifle and charged down the side of the peak and into the fiery and swirling dervish of death. If there was anyone left in that camp still alive, they wouldn't be much longer.

Chapter 15

When the smoke and dust cleared, Longarm could see bodies everywhere, and some of them were just in small parts. However, it appeared that some of the men had been some distance away from the campfire when the dynamite exploded, and these men were still alive, although dazed and injured.

Longarm had no choice except to try to keep them alive. There were four men who stood a good chance of making it, and two others who were so severely injured by the blast that they were dying.

"Zellner?" Longarm asked, staring down at what physically remained of the rancher. "Is that really you?"

"My arm!" the man groaned. "It's gone!"

It was missing from the elbow on down. One side of Zellner's face was burned black, and his lips looked like pieces of charred meat when he whispered, "Help me! Don't let me die!"

Longarm found rope and knotted a tourniquet around Zellner's stump, which immediately staunched the bleeding. Zellner grabbed Longarm by the sleeve and hissed, "Save me and I'll make sure you get rich!"

"I've got others to help," Longarm told the man as he removed his talonlike grip. "I'll be back."

"No!"

But Longarm left the rancher and hurried about helping a few others who had not been instantly killed in the explosion. Two of the survivors had been off tending to the mules, which had all run away a short distance and were now wildly braying in the moonlight. After disarming this dazed pair, Longarm said, "You're both under arrest."

The men were so stunned and in shock that it was obvious they wouldn't be dangerous. Longarm located another man who was still clutching his Winchester. Longarm knew this was the marksman assigned to shoot him if he had attempted to sneak out of the mine tunnel.

"Are you all right?" Longarm asked.

The man didn't answer.

"How bad are you hurt?"

When the man still said nothing, Longarm leaned closer to see that a walnut-sized rock had struck the man in the chest and pierced his heart.

Longarm finished his rounds, and then he dragged and carried Zellner and the other survivors over to what had earlier been their campfire. He fed the fire with wood until its flames rose ten feet high because he needed more light to try to doctor the survivors.

Zellner was the most seriously injured. He was moaning and in intense pain. Ed Gill, the other rancher and conspirator, must have been very near the explosion because Longarm could not identify his remains.

"I'm going to die," Zellner moaned, his face a sickly gray color in the firelight. "I'm going to die, aren't I?"

"I don't know," Longarm told the man, although he was sure that Zellner wasn't going to last through the night. "Where is your whiskey? It might help you hold on until morning."

"Over there," Zellner whispered, pointing. "Behind those rocks you'll find our food and drink."

Longarm hurried over to the whiskey, needing a stiff drink of his own. He upended the bottle, taking four or five big swallows and thinking that if he'd have tossed the fourth stick of dynamite, every last man in this camp would have been obliterated by the blast.

Longarm brought whiskey to the survivors, but two of them, both miners, didn't seem to understand what they were being offered. Zellner, however, drank a generous amount, then sat rocking back and forth on his haunches weeping like an old man knowing that he was about to die.

"I won't make it," he said. "You're not a doctor! I'm missing my arm and I'm sure as hell gonna die."

"It doesn't help to think that way," Longarm told the man. "At first light, if you're still alive, I'll catch up the mules, hitch 'em to a wagon, and take what's left of you back to Montezuma."

Zellner rolled his head from side to side. "Not Montezuma. Take us to Santa Fe where they've got some good doctors."

"Okay," Longarm said agreeably. "We'll strike out for Santa Fe, but first you're going to tell me everything you know about the Montezuma murders."

Even though he was in agony, Zellner's face twisted

with hatred and he hissed, "Go to hell, Marshal! I ain't tellin' you anything!"

"If that's the way you feel," Longarm said, "then I might as well let you bleed to death right now and be done with you."

He reached over and pretended that he was going to untie the tourniquet located just above Zellner's elbow.

"No!" the rancher screamed. "If you take that off, I'll bleed out in minutes."

"Zellner, it's your choice," Longarm said. "Talk or bleed out, it is all the same to me."

Zellner's eyebrows and eyelashes were burned away. He blinked back fresh tears and blurted out, "All right! You already know that Doug Ward and Mrs. Trotter are behind all the murders. They came to me and Ed . . . my God! Where is Ed Gill?"

"The explosion blew him to smithereens, so I'd guess that he's probably burning in hell," Longarm said without a hint of sympathy.

Zellner wept even harder. Finally, Longarm prodded him with the neck of the whiskey bottle. "Why don't you have another stout pull on this and then tell me everything. If you do, I promise I'll do my level best to deliver you to a Santa Fe doctor. If you cooperate with the prosecution and prove yourself to be a good witness, then you might get off with a light prison sentence and live long enough to see your ranch again. It's your choice, Zellner."

When the man hesitated, Longarm reached for the tourniquet again, and Zellner cried out, "No! I'll talk. Just promise to save me."

Longarm knew that he had to get the answers right now because this man was almost certainly going to die before morning. "Listen," Longarm said, "I'm no doctor, but I'll do all that I can to get you to Santa Fe still breathing. But in exchange for that, you have to tell me everything about the murders. That's the deal. Take it or leave it."

"I'll tell you," Zellner promised. "Tell you everything."

"Then start at the beginning," Longarm ordered.

"Okay. But first, can I have another pull on that bottle? I'm in terrible pain, Marshal."

"Talk awhile. If I think you're telling me the truth, I'll give you another drink," Longarm promised.

Zellner closed his eyes and shuddered. Finally, he said, "A few months ago a prospector came to us saying that he had discovered a vein of pure gold. He was an old fool and wanted whiskey and a lot of money before he told us exactly where the gold was found. We'd grubstaked the man in the past and knew he wouldn't be lying outright."

"*Who* grubstaked him?" Longarm asked.

"Me and Ed Gill."

"And then what happened?"

"We gave the man a hundred dollars and a couple of bottles of whiskey. He got roaring drunk and told us about finding gold on the side of Diablo Peak. Ed and I rode over and when we saw the vein, we knew the strike was worth a fortune."

"Then what did you do about the drunken prospector?"

Zellner swallowed hard. "We paid him some more and told him to ride out of the territory and never say a word about the strike on Diablo Peak."

137

"You're lying," Longarm snapped. "You'd never have allowed him to go, so you killed the man."

"Ed killed him! I didn't!"

Longarm didn't believe that for a minute, but since Ed Gill was dead, there was really no way to prove that Zellner was lying, so he said, "Go on."

"Ed figured he had to kill that prospector or the man would have blabbed about the strike to everyone. Ed and I both realized right off that Diablo Peak was on public land and, if we filed a mining claim, *everyone* would want a piece of Diablo . . . including the damned Zuni Indians."

"And they had a claim to it?" Longarm asked.

"Sure! They were already getting some sympathetic support in Santa Fe and were pushing a claim on Diablo Peak based on their religious rituals."

"But wouldn't they be watching you when you started digging those tunnels and make a fuss?"

"We shot them whenever they came around, and buried their bodies up in that first mine tunnel we dug to the right of the one you were hiding in. We knew that we couldn't let the damned Zuni make a big fuss over our illegal mining on public land."

"You were biding time and hoping to get the support of the vice president during his upcoming visit."

"Yeah." Zellner grimaced. "I need more whiskey!"

Longarm gave him three long swallows, then placed the whiskey just out of his reach. Longarm was getting everything he needed to know. If Zellner could hang on a little longer and tell him the rest, he'd have this case solved.

"What about Doug Ward and Mrs. Trotter?" Longarm asked. "How did they fit into this scheme?"

Zellner was failing. His breathing was coming harder, but now that he was talking, he seemed to want to get out the whole story. "Ward and Mrs. Trotter have the connections to reach the vice president. They know all the right people in Santa Fe and they aren't afraid of asking for political favors."

Longarm nodded. "So they were going to be the ones to get the vice president to shut out the Zuni and somehow turn Diablo Peak into private property. Private property that you, Ed Gill, Doug Ward, and Mrs. Trotter could buy cheap, and then realize a fortune in gold."

"Yeah," Zellner wheezed. "We knew that there was a good chance that the vice president would award us the land and shut out the Zuni if the right strings were pulled."

"But that isn't going to happen now," Longarm said harshly.

"We almost pulled it off," Zellner said, his fingers trying to reach the whiskey. "We would have made it if you'd stayed in Denver."

"How many Zuni were shot?"

"Maybe four or five."

Longarm was filled with contempt. "You murdered a lot of good white people and Zuni. All for nothing!"

"More whiskey!"

"Not yet," Longarm said, now wanting this man to suffer and then die after he finished his murderous tale. "I want to know who actually killed the past mayor, the marshal, and those two city councilmen."

"Ed Gill and I shot the Indians. But for the others, we hired two professional gunmen. Once they did what we wanted, Ed and I ambushed them not a mile from here."

"Where are their bodies to be found?"

Zellner glanced up Diablo Peak. "In the other tunnel that we worked out and then filled in with rocks so that the bodies would never be found."

"Anything else you have to tell me?"

Zellner shook his head. "Ed and I both got crazy with gold fever. Once the killing started, we couldn't see any way to stop until there was no one except the four of us left . . . and both Ed and I figured that we were going to have to kill Doug Ward and the widow woman before it was all finished."

"You don't deserve to live," Longarm told the man.

Zellner looked up at him, and there were tears in his eyes. "It was the gold that made us so crazy. I'd never have killed Ed because he was my best friend. My only friend! You know, he had a wife and four good kids. Ed had himself a real nice family! You made his wife a widow, Marshal! And all those kids won't have a father anymore."

"I expect Mrs. Gill and her children will survive just fine. They have a big ranch, don't they? What about you, Zellner? If you don't make it to Santa Fe, who are you leaving behind?"

"I don't have family. My wife left me years ago and took my boys to California."

"Maybe she somehow guessed you'd kill a lot of people for gold," Longarm said.

"If I make it to Santa Fe and a doctor saves me," Zellner said, "I wouldn't be sentenced to hang, would I?"

"I don't know," Longarm said. "You've told me the truth, haven't you?"

"I swear I have!" Zellner took a couple of deep

140

breaths. "But I feel like I'm slipping away, Marshal. I feel like I'm dying and I'm gawdamn scared!"

"Just keep breathing," Longarm said, having no sympathy at all for this man.

Zellner tried to reach out and grab the whiskey. "Another drink! I need another drink to keep me goin', Marshal! I've told you everything I know, now give me more whiskey!"

But Longarm shook his head.

Zellner's face suddenly twisted in a last spasm of hatred. "You coldhearted sonofabitch!"

Longarm snorted with contempt and started to leave. "You call *me* coldhearted? Zellner, you're the one that's earned a one-way ticket to hell."

Zellner tried to curse him, but instead died choking.

"Good riddance," Longarm said, thinking about how satisfying it would be to arrest Mayor Doug Ward and Mrs. Trotter. Once he'd done that, justice would finally have been served for the Montezuma murders.

Chapter 16

Longarm caught the spooky mules after they'd finally settled down. He then hitched up a wagon to carry in the bodies and those who survived but were wounded in the dynamite explosion. The hard-rock miners were subdued, scared, and filled with remorse. All of them swore to Longarm that they'd had no part in any of the murders.

"We're just hardworking men and we were paid well to mine the vein of gold and keep our mouths shut about it. Hell, Marshal, they didn't even let us go to town for fear that the news of this gold strike would get out before they got ownership of the land. We were here most all the time, or they kept us hidden on Zellner's ranch."

"I believe you," Longarm said, "but you men must have been aware of the bodies that were being put into those two extra tunnels."

"They were put there by Mr. Gill and Mr. Zellner," one of the miners explained. "And we were warned that, if we ever breathed a word of what we saw here, we'd all be shot and buried in those same Diablo Peak tunnels."

One of the miners was so badly wounded that he couldn't climb into the back of the wagon, so Longarm said to his friends, "Help him up in there and we'll go to Santa Fe and find a doctor."

"Marshal, will we *hang*?" a miner asked, his eyes wide and round with fear.

Longarm thought about his answer for a moment, then said, "Not if you cooperate with the investigation and any trial that might take place. Zellner was going to be my main witness, but as you know, he didn't make it."

"Zellner and Gill were the ones behind the killings," a miner said. "We'll all swear in a court of law to that!"

The others nodded in vigorous agreement.

Longarm had another question to ask. "Did any of you see Doug Ward and the Widow Trotter come here to Diablo Peak?"

"Sure!" one of them said. "They came a bunch of times. They had the gold fever even worse than Mr. Zellner and Mr. Gill."

"And were they here when bodies were buried in those tunnels?"

"Not every time, they weren't. But a couple of times when Zuni were brought in dead, they were here and didn't object."

"That's all I needed to know," Longarm said as he climbed up into the wagon box and took the lines. "And that's all that you need to tell a judge in order for them both to hang, or at least spend the rest of their lives in a prison."

"Will someone dig out those two tunnels and bring down all the bodies hidden inside?" a miner asked.

"I expect someone will do that right away."

"They used dynamite to close those two tunnels," another miner explained. "But I don't think that you'd have to clear more than ten feet of rock to reach the bodies. We could help on that, if it would maybe go in our favor when we stand before a judge."

"I'll make your offer known," Longarm said. "Everyone aboard?"

"Yes, sir!"

"Hang on. This will be a rough trip to town, and I'll push these mules just as hard as I can."

Longarm slapped the mules on the rump and reined them away from the camp toward where he'd hidden the blue roan. Once that animal was retrieved and tied to the back of the wagon, they headed straight for Santa Fe.

When Longarm reached Santa Fe, he tied up in front of the local marshal's office and helped his injured prisoners into the man's small and untidy front room.

Marshal Wade Duncan was a large-bellied man in his fifties, and when he saw the blackened faces and torn clothes, he came to his feet with a start. "My gawd! What is going on here?"

Longarm introduced himself and explained what had happened at Diablo Peak. He ended by saying, "I was trapped in a tunnel partway up Diablo Peak where these men were mining gold for Doug Ward, Ed Gill, Ben Zellner, and Mrs. Linda Trotter."

"Diablo Peak is on *government* land."

"I know that," Longarm replied. "And they all knew it, too. But they'd murdered a prospector who discovered gold on the peak, and they were trying to get as much of the vein out as possible. To do that they hired these miners, a couple of gunmen, and some others that didn't make it. They were also angling to get the vice president's ear when he arrives here in order to have Diablo Peak changed to private ownership."

The marshal acted as if he could not quite believe everything he'd just been told. "You got any proof of this?" he finally asked.

"All the proof we need," Longarm assured him. "And these are my star witnesses to all the murders."

Marshal Duncan blew out a lungful of air and scratched his head. "I'd like to see your badge."

Longarm showed it to him, and Duncan said, "So you're a federal officer, huh?"

"That's right. I was sent from Denver to see if I could put a stop to the murders and arrest the guilty."

"So you arrested these miners?"

Longarm was beginning to suspect that Marshal Duncan was not overly bright. Either that, or he was party to the murders. "Listen, Marshal," Longarm said with growing impatience, "these men all need to see a doctor. I don't think they're killers, but you should lock them up and have a doctor treat them in your jail cell until I'm sure that there are no loose ends to this case."

Duncan said, "I don't know if you're aware of it, but Ed Gill and Ben Zellner are influential ranchers in this part of the country. I expect they'll say you're about as wrong as wrong can be."

"Not likely," Longarm replied. "Zellner's body is still in the wagon, and there isn't enough of Ed Gill left to fill a coffee cup."

Marshal Duncan's square jaw dropped with amazement. "They're *both* dead?"

"That's right. And now, if you'll put these injured miners in your jail cell, I'm going to find and arrest Mrs. Trotter."

Duncan nodded, but didn't move.

"What?" Longarm asked, starting to get angry.

"Mrs. Trotter left town yesterday. I saw her board the stagecoach for Montezuma."

Longarm swore under his breath. "Then I'd better ride for Montezuma. My guess is that I'll find her with Douglas Ward. If I do, I'll arrest the both of them and bring them back here to stand trial for murder."

"Now, wait a minute!" Duncan protested. "Doug Ward is the acting mayor of Montezuma. He and Mrs. Trotter have a lot of important friends here in Santa Fe, and I can't just toss them into jail without some proof that they're guilty. And frankly, Marshal, despite what you claim, I ain't all that sure they're really guilty."

Longarm suddenly understood what he was up against. Marshal Duncan was in cahoots with the rest of them, and was desperately trying to find a way to get out of this mess without being caught up in the Montezuma murders. And yet, none of the miners had said anything about ever having seen the Santa Fe marshal out at Diablo Peak.

"Tell you what," Longarm said, now choosing his words with care. "I'll go to Montezuma and arrest Mr. Ward and Mrs. Trotter. In the meantime, you—"

"I'm coming with you," Duncan suddenly decided. "Those two are important people, and I don't trust you to take them alive."

"What about these men I arrested and brought here for medical treatment?" Longarm asked.

"We'll get a doctor over here to examine them," Duncan promised. "And I've got a deputy that can watch 'em while we're gone."

"You don't have any authority in Montezuma," Longarm told the man. "You're the town marshal of Santa Fe."

"I don't give a damn about that!" Duncan erupted angrily. "I've known Doug and Linda since they were kids, and I just don't believe they are capable of murder."

"Then you don't know them very well at all," Longarm snapped.

"I'm coming," Marshal Duncan insisted. "I don't trust you. Why, you've still got a stick of dynamite in your coat pocket!"

Longarm looked down and realized this was true. "I only needed three out of four."

Duncan shook his head. "I'm going to telegraph Denver and make sure that you really are who you say you are."

"Fine," Longarm said, "but do it fast, because I'm sure that Douglas Ward and Mrs. Trotter already have heard about what took place at Diablo Peak and they're not going to wait around for me to put them in handcuffs."

Longarm headed outside. He also needed to send a telegram to Denver. Billy Vail would be extremely anxious about what was taking place here in New Mexico, and Longarm sure had a lot to tell the man. And with any luck at all, he'd have this murder case wrapped up and soon be on his way back to Denver, Colorado.

Chapter 17

Longarm sent his telegram off to Denver explaining everything that he'd discovered, and he ended the message by saying that he thought that the marshal of Santa Fe, Wade Duncan, might be involved in the conspiracy and that they were on their way together to Montezuma for a showdown.

"That ought to do it," he said, handing the telegram to the operator. "Send it out immediately."

The operator read the message, and his face showed his astonishment and disbelief. "Marshal, are you sure you want to send this?"

"Of course I do," Longarm told the man. "And if you breathe a word of it to anyone—and I mean anyone—then I'll see that you go to jail for a long, long time. Is that understood?"

The man nodded. "I just can't believe that Marshal Duncan would be a part of anything illegal."

"Well," Longarm told the man, "maybe he isn't. It's just a hunch, and I'll find out if it's right or wrong as soon as we reach Montezuma."

"Yes, sir!"

Longarm paid the man for the telegram and headed up the street, stopping in at the jail to check on the injured miners once more. A young doctor was in the cell with them. He had his black leather medical kit open and was working feverishly on the miners.

"Are they all going to live, Doc?" Longarm asked through the bars.

"No thanks to you," the doctor replied. "My God, what kind of a lawman is it that throws dynamite into a campfire!"

"A lawman that had no other options if he expected to survive," Longarm answered. "Keep them alive, Doc. They're going on the witness stand and I need them all to testify."

The doctor shot Longarm a stern look of disapproval and turned back to minister to his jailed patients.

Longarm didn't wait around. He checked up and down the street seeking Marshal Duncan, but didn't see the lawman. Longarm was famished, so he went into a small Mexican café and had a big meal of fried beans, beef, and tortillas, washing it all down with good beer. When he reappeared in the street, Duncan was coming to meet him leading his horse.

"I'm ready to ride if you are," Duncan said, glancing up at the darkening sky. "But I think we're in for some bad weather. Maybe we should wait until tomorrow."

"I'm not waiting," Longarm answered. He untied his roan from the back of the wagon and swung into the saddle. "Let's ride."

* * *

150

They'd kept up a steady pace for mile after mile and it was getting late in the day. Longarm was weary, but determined to finish up this murder case as soon as possible. The weather was getting worse and the wind was really starting to blow down from the north.

"Long," the marshal from Santa Fe said, "it'll be dark in a few minutes and no matter how hard we push, we still can't reach Montezuma before midnight. I know a man who has a little homestead not far away and he'll put us up for the night. What do you say? We could get up early and still be in Montezuma before noon."

Longarm was very tempted by this suggestion. His blue roan was worn down and was long overdue to be fed. The animal looked as if it had lost a hundred pounds since he'd rented it from Jake's Stable only a few days earlier.

"You say he's a homesteader?"

"That's right. He runs a few head of cattle and horses. Takes in travelers and runs a trapline. He's a good man. Name is Art Hiller. He'll feed us and the horses and give us a place to get in out of this foul weather."

Longarm had been hearing the approaching thunder, and knew that they were riding straight into the path of a fierce lightning storm. It wasn't real smart to do that, so he said, "All right. Lead the way."

Marshal Duncan reined his horse off the main road and onto a little wagon track leading off to the east. Soon, rain began to splatter the dust, and as darkness fell, white lightning shivered brilliantly across the dark sky.

"Let's move out faster!" Marshal Duncan yelled into the storm, which was starting to pelt them with cold, heavy raindrops.

Longarm gave the roan its head, and the animal followed Marshal Duncan's horse up the wagon track at a fast gallop. By now, it was getting so dark and stormy that it was nearly impossible to see where they were going, but Longarm knew the roan could see well enough to run.

On and on they galloped, sometimes almost getting swept out of their saddles by low-hanging limbs. Once, the roan slipped in mud and nearly tumbled, but Longarm jerked the animal's head up and they kept running with lightning now striking nearby treetops.

At last, Longarm heard the frantic barking of ranch dogs, and they burst out of the heavy forest into a clearing before a log cabin. He smelled smoke and meat frying. The ranch dogs kept barking until a jolt of lightning sent them running for cover under the cabin's front porch.

"Barn's over here!" Marshal Duncan yelled in the downpour. "Come along!"

Longarm followed the marshal, and saw another man standing by a barn with the door held open. He galloped the roan straight into the barn, and it was like emerging from under a waterfall.

"Sure is comin' down like cats and dogs!" the homesteader shouted. "What the hell are you fellas doin' out in such a bad storm!"

Marshal Duncan was so stiff and cold that he nearly fell off his horse onto the ground, but managed to stay erect by grabbing his saddle horn.

"You all right?" the homesteader asked.

"Sure," Duncan said, wiping the rain from his face and then gesturing toward Longarm. "This is Deputy United States Marshal Custis Long from Denver."

"What the deuce are you doin' out here all the way from Denver?" the man asked. He was a short, wiry man who had bib overalls, heavy work boots, and a thick black beard crusted with grease.

"The usual," Longarm replied, stepping down from his horse and then throwing back his stirrup so that he could loosen the cinch and unsaddle the exhausted blue roan.

"You can put the roan in that stall and, Marshal Duncan, you put your horse in that other stall," the man instructed. "I'll get them a good bait of grain and plenty of hay. Those horses look plain worn out."

"We've been traveling hard," Longarm explained. "I rented this animal from Jake Fernley over in Montezuma. I don't think he's going to be too happy about the condition I'm returning him in."

Art Hiller scoffed. "Jake will give you hell and he'll charge you a few dollars extra, but that horse will come back strong as soon as he's fed up and rested a few days. He appears to be a fine, young gelding."

"He is," Longarm agreed. "How much do you charge for putting us up for the night?"

"A dollar for you and your horse. Includes your meal and a little whiskey if you are good company."

"Fair enough," Longarm said, whipping the rain off his hat.

Hiller said, "I got some good beef stew on the fire and plenty of hot coffee to wash it down with."

Longarm smiled and listened to the storm batter the barn until it almost shook. He said to Marshal Duncan, "Good idea to come here."

"You're damn right!" the marshal of Santa Fe exclaimed as he unsaddled his own horse. "A man can get fried to a cinder by lightning or catch his death of pneumonia while being out in this bad weather. Let's go inside and get warmed up by the fireplace."

"Go on ahead," Art Hiller called as he led the horses to their stalls. "I'll get these horses fed and watered and be right in myself. Pour yourselves some hot coffee, too!"

Longarm was a good judge of men, and he judged that Hiller was not someone he had to worry about, so he nodded and said, "Much obliged."

Once inside the cabin, they pulled off their soggy coats and placed them on antler racks fixed to Hiller's wall not far from the crackling potbellied stove, so they'd be dry in the morning. The cabin was only two rooms and not especially large. Longarm figured he would sleep on the floor tonight, and that was all right so long as he was warm and dry. Sleeping on wooden planks might leave him a bit stiff and sore tomorrow morning, but he'd manage.

"Coffee?" Duncan said, grabbing up a couple of tin cups and reaching for the pot.

"Sure," Longarm replied, eyeing the pot of bubbling stew. "Does Hiller make a good meal?"

"He does," the marshal said. "And he makes some corn liquor that is the real reason people stop here for the night."

"Might try some," Longarm said.

Art Hiller came to join them a few minutes later. He stomped mud off his boots and shrugged out of his coat. "Fed and grained those horses. They'll look and feel a lot better by morning, same as you fellas. Dish up some of that stew. There's bowls and spoons on the counter."

"How about some of that good corn liquor?" Marshal Duncan said. "Or have you drunk it all since I was here last time?"

"I got plenty left," Hiller told them. And to prove it, he found a jug and said, "Drink down that coffee and let me add a little jolt to it."

Longarm did as the man suggested, and the "jolt" of whiskey warmed him right down to the bottom of his belly.

"There," Hiller said, looking proud of himself. "Now you fellas got some color back in your cheeks. When you rode into that barn, you were both white as ghosts."

Longarm sipped his coffee and looked the cabin over. It was humble and untidy, filled with traps, saddles, and harness in various stages of mending. It looked like what it was, a bachelor's homestead.

"So what brings you out here in this kind of weather?" Hiller asked, taking a pull on the jug.

Duncan looked over at Longarm and said, "I'd better let him tell you because I don't believe it myself."

Longarm sipped at his coffee and stood closer to the fire. He didn't really feel like telling this man about the gold and bodies in Diablo Peak, but he knew he owed Art Hiller some kind of explanation, so he said, "I've been sent from Denver to see about the Montezuma murders. I think we have a lead and we're going to Montezuma to make a couple of arrests."

"You mean to say that you know who did all them terrible murders?" Hiller's excitement was plain. "Holy smokes! I'm dyin' to know!"

"I can't tell you just yet," Longarm said. "But I suppose you knew Ben Zellner and Ed Gill."

"Sure! They buy a couple jugs of my corn liquor whenever they're passin' this way."

"Well," Longarm said, "they won't be doin' that anymore because I blew them up yesterday with dynamite."

The homesteader gaped. "You . . . you killed Ed and Ben?"

"Yeah," Longarm said. "They were part of the bunch that has been murdering so many people around here."

"But why? They both owned a lot of land and cattle. Those two had plenty of money. What did they need to kill anyone for?"

"It's a long story," Longarm told the man, "but the sad truth is few people believe they ever have enough money. Rich people included."

"Holy smokes! I . . . I still can't believe what you're tellin' me." Hiller took another pull on the jug and, without asking, poured more whiskey into Longarm's and Duncan's coffee. "So tell me why Ben and Ed would do anything so bad that they needed to be killed."

Longarm saw no way to avoid telling the man about the gold strike on Diablo Peak. And about Mrs. Linda Trotter and Doug Ward. He ended up by saying, "The assayer in Montezuma, Thad Walker, told me that the gold is high-grade, so it's just a matter of the size of the vein of gold. The strike could be worth hundreds of thousands, but it could also peter out in a hurry."

"And that's what was behind all those murders?" Art

Hiller asked, still shaking his head with disbelief and shifting his gaze back and forth between Longarm and the marshal of Santa Fe.

"That's the reason," Longarm said. "We've got witnesses locked up in Marshal Duncan's jail back in Santa Fe, and they'll testify in order to avoid serving time in prison. All that is left is to arrest Mayor Ward and Mrs. Trotter for murder."

Hiller turned to Marshal Duncan. "Can this be true, Marshal Duncan?"

"I don't know," the man said. "But time will tell."

"Holy smokes," the homesteader said, taking another long pull on his jug of corn liquor. "It just makes you wonder who you can trust these days."

"Isn't that a fact," Marshal Duncan said, with his back turned to them. Suddenly, he drew his gun and pointed it at Longarm and repeated, "It seems that you just can't trust anyone anymore."

Longarm knew that there was no way he could draw his gun before Duncan shot him to death. He was holding a cup of coffee in one hand and a spoon in the other, and he momentarily thought of hurling both toward the marshal, but knew that wasn't going to work either.

"I never trusted you from the first," Longarm told the marshal from Santa Fe. "And now I know that you were in on the murders right from the start."

"Sure I was," Duncan said. "Who in their right mind would turn down the chance to become rich?"

"Marshal Duncan," the homesteader cried. "You can't be serious. Tell me that you're makin' a joke!"

"It's no joke," Longarm told the homesteader. "And the next question is, what is he going to do about us?"

Duncan frowned. "Ed and Ben are dead, so that lessens the number of slices out of the pie. I don't suppose that I could pay you enough money to keep quiet about all this? You know, just both of you disappear?"

"I would," Art Hiller choked. "You wouldn't kill me, would you? I'm your friend!"

"He doesn't have any friends," Longarm explained. "And he can't afford to let you live now that he's decided to kill me. Isn't that right?"

"I'm afraid it is," Duncan said, cocking his six-gun. "But for your information, I didn't personally kill anyone. It was all done by professionals that were hired and . . . and eliminated."

"And their bodies can be found on Diablo Peak?" Longarm asked.

"Yep."

Art Hiller was slowly coming to understand that he was about to be shot to death. He began to shake and then plead. "Listen, Marshal Duncan, you can trust me not to say anything. Honest! I'll stay right here and I don't want any gold or anything. Just come on by and share a jug when you're thirsty and—"

"Shut up!" Duncan ordered. "This isn't what I wanted, but Marshal Long here insisted we strike out for Montezuma. So I had no choice but to go along and then wait for the chance to kill him. Art, you just happened to be in the wrong place at the wrong time."

"No!" the homesteader cried, jumping for a rifle that was leaning against a nearby wall.

Longarm saw his chance. As Duncan swung his pistol and fired at the homesteader, Longarm made a stab for his six-gun. But Duncan was faster than expected, and he shot Hiller and then turned his gun on Longarm, saying, "Freeze or you're dead!"

Longarm's hand was on the butt of his gun, but it was still only halfway out of his holster. He knew that, if he continued his play, the marshal would shoot him where he stood.

"Smart," Duncan told him. "Now raise your hands and back up against the wall nice and slow."

Longarm raised his hands, and Duncan stepped forward and snatched his Colt from its holster, then retreated a few steps.

"Well, well," Marshal Duncan said, "it seems that we have a situation here."

"Yeah," Longarm said, desperately trying to figure out a way to survive. His only hope seemed to be the little double-barreled derringer that rested in his vest and was affixed to his gold watch chain.

"You know," Duncan told him, "it's too bad that I'm going to have to kill you."

"Oh," Longarm said cryptically, "I don't think it's going to cause you to lose any sleep. I imagine you've killed a lot of men and never gave it a second thought."

"I've killed more than a few that well deserved it."

"Well, I don't deserve it and neither did poor Hiller. He thought you were his friend."

Longarm was hoping that the marshal might glance back at the dead homesteader and give him a chance to go for his hideout derringer, but Duncan was too wise for that. He kept his eyes and his gun dead center on Longarm.

"You'll be the second lawman that I've had to deal with, and that troubles me."

"The first being poor Marshal Homer Wilson?"

"Yeah," Duncan said. "Of course, I wasn't in the saloon that night so I didn't put the knife to Homer, but I had to hire the man that did."

"And that bothers you?"

"Of course! Homer was a fine, earnest young man. He just wasn't too smart."

Longarm lowered his hands a fraction. "You'll never get away with this, Duncan. It's gone too far."

"I disagree. You've eliminated Ed Gill and Ben Zellner along with others. So now it's just me, Linda, and Doug Ward." Marshal Duncan smiled. "If I go on to Montezuma tomorrow morning, I'll figure out a way to eliminate them and then I can have the Diablo Peak gold to myself."

Longarm shook his head. "Aren't you forgetting about those miners that are in your jail?"

"They are easily expendable. A jailbreak, I think. Yes, they tried to break out and I had no choice but to shoot them down."

"That's a stretch. What about me?"

"Oh," Duncan said, "your death is easily explained. You and poor Art Hiller were drinking and got into a fight. He shot you and then died from your gun."

Longarm almost laughed. "You really think people are going to believe that?"

"Why not? I've been a model lawman in Santa Fe. They don't want to lose me, so they'll believe exactly what I tell them."

Longarm could see that the man had it all figured out in his sick mind and that he himself had moments left to live. "Mind if I check the time?"

160

"What for?" Duncan asked.

Longarm thought quickly. "A fortune-teller once looked into her crystal ball and predicted I'd die at ten o'clock in the evening. I think it is about that time right now."

"Hmmm," Duncan said. "I've always sort of believed in fortune-tellers. Had my own fortune read a few times."

"And did it say that you would become rich?" Longarm asked, playing for time.

"As a matter of fact, it did. And I think that prediction will soon be coming true."

"How about I check my pocket watch and see if it's ten o'clock?"

"By all means, do that," Duncan said. "It'll be your last wish granted."

Longarm reached under his coat and into his vest pocket. His fingers found the deadly little derringer, and he drew it out in one swift motion, firing the instant the barrels were lined up on Duncan's chest.

The explosion was deafening and Marshal Duncan was caught off guard. He staggered backward, face contorted with surprise, shock, and absolute confusion.

"Why, you—"

Longarm jumped forward and batted the man's gun aside, and then threw him across the room even as the light was dying in Duncan's eyes.

When the marshal of Santa Fe crashed to the floor of the cabin twitching in death, Longarm stepped over to him and said, "I guess neither one of us should have believed in fortune-tellers, huh?"

Duncan didn't hear that, but it didn't matter. The

man was dead, and now there were only two people left to find and either kill or arrest. Mayor Douglas Ward and Mrs. Linda Trotter.

Longarm went over and knelt beside the home-steader's body. "You didn't deserve this," he told the dead man. "And if your spirit doesn't mind, I think I'll drink a toast to you with your good corn liquor and then go to bed. In the morning, I'll take your body and that of the marshal into Montezuma and see that you get a decent burial, but not Marshal Duncan."

Having said this, Longarm found the jug, raised a toast to poor Art Hiller, and drank the fiery corn liquor until it was all gone.

Chapter 18

People stopped in the streets when Longarm rode into Montezuma leading two horses with dead men strapped across their saddles. He dismounted and tied his blue roan and the other two horses at the hitching rail in front of the town's only funeral parlor.

"Ain't this the marshal of Santa Fe?" the undertaker asked a few minutes later while lifting up the man's head and staring at the dead face.

"Yep," Longarm said. "His name is—or was—Marshal Wade Duncan."

The undertaker shook his head. "This New Mexico Territory sure is hell on marshals, isn't it?"

"Yes, it is," Longarm agreed.

"Who shot him?"

"I did."

The undertaker blinked and took a step back. "*You* shot Santa Fe's town marshal?"

"Yep. And he shot the other man, whose name is Art Hiller. Hiller owned a little homestead about twenty miles from here."

The undertaker looked at the smaller man. "I've seen Hiller in town getting supplies a time or two. He was unkempt, but he really seemed like a nice enough fella."

"He was," Longarm agreed.

"Did you also shoot Mr. Hiller?"

"No. The dead marshal shot Hiller. Then I shot the marshal. Got it?"

"I believe I do," the undertaker said, trying to maintain his composure. "Who's going to pay for their funeral expenses?"

"Beats me," Longarm replied.

"Does either man have family?"

"I have no idea."

"Well," the undertaker said, "I don't work for free. There are expenses I have to pay for in addition to my professional services. I'm going to need to know who will reimburse me."

Longarm thought about that for a moment. His mind was totally focused on catching Ward and Trotter, but he could see the reasonableness of this man's concerns, so he said, "How about you take the horses, saddles, guns, and gear and sell them. That ought to more than cover the expenses. But this blue roan belongs to Jake Fernley. So he's not part of the deal. Understand?"

"I understand." The undertaker, a slight man in his early thirties, expertly studied the horses carrying the bodies. "The marshal's horse has a rifle, does it go with the deal?"

"Yes," Longarm told him. "So are we square?"

"I expect so," the undertaker said. "The rifle, saddles, and horses will actually more than cover the burial expenses."

"Give the extra money to the most worthy local char-ity," Longarm suggested.

"I can and will do exactly that. But do you mind telling me why you shot the marshal of Santa Fe?"

Longarm loosened the cinch on the blue roan and noted that it looked pretty worn out. "It's a long story and one I haven't got the time to tell. Right now, I'm looking for your mayor, Douglas Ward."

"Are you planning to shoot him, too?"

"That all depends," Longarm answered. "Have you seen him or Mrs. Trotter around town today?"

"As a matter of fact, I did see them this morning."

"Where?"

The undertaker frowned. "Marshal, given as how I consider them friends, I'm not sure that I want to tell you."

Longarm understood. "Never mind. If they're in town, I'll find them soon enough."

"I've only got two caskets. And I'll be using them for Mr. Duncan and Mr. Hiller. If you're going to kill our mayor and Mrs. Trotter, I've got to get my carpenter working on more caskets immediately. I really need to know if you're going to kill them both next!"

Longarm hesitated. "I'm going to try and arrest them," he told the undertaker. "But if they resist, then I'll have to get serious."

"Meaning you'll shoot them dead?"

"That's how I usually do it," Longarm said matter-of-factly before walking away.

He went directly to Montezuma's city hall and asked about Mayor Ward. The woman at the front desk said,

"He had to leave on a personal emergency this morning."

"What *kind* of emergency?"

"Mayor Ward didn't say and I didn't feel it my place to ask."

"Did he say when he'd return?"

"No." She was trying not to look irritated by Longarm's direct and personal questions. "Is there something important that you need to say to Mr. Ward? Or perhaps you could leave a written message and I'll make sure that it's delivered just as soon as he returns."

"Thanks, but no, thanks," Longarm replied. "Where does he live?"

"Up the street at the Santa Fe Hotel. But—"

Longarm tipped his hat to the woman. "Much obliged."

He knew where the Santa Fe Hotel was, and he hoped that he could catch Douglas Ward and Mrs. Trotter before they disappeared. Longarm was quite sure that they had already learned about the trouble at Diablo Peak and the huge dynamite explosion. That meant that they would know they were in serious trouble and that their involvement in the murders was very likely about to be exposed. They would have no choice but to go on the run with whatever cash or gold they could grab in a hurry, and Longarm knew they wouldn't stop running for a long, long time.

Longarm entered the Santa Fe Hotel, which was an extremely impressive two-story adobe building whose lobby had beautiful tile floors. A fountain bubbled in the center of the lobby and four massive chandeliers overhead were made of heavy, black Spanish iron. Longarm's boot heels clicked on the polished tiles as walked briskly over to speak to a man who looked like he might be the hotel's manager.

"I'm looking for Mayor Ward," he said. "Do you know if he's in his room?"

"I'm sure he is not," the man replied. "I saw him depart less than two hours ago."

"Did he say where he was going?"

"I think he was leaving on the stagecoach."

"What makes you think that?" Longarm demanded.

"I saw a ticket in his hand." The man frowned. "May I ask why you want to know?"

"No, you may not," Longarm said as he was leaving.

He hurried down the street, cutting quickly across the plaza to reach the town's only stagecoach yard and office. Barging inside, he asked the man working at a desk, "I'm looking for Mayor Ward and Mrs. Trotter. Did they take the stage out of town yet?"

"Oh, yes."

"And their destination?"

"Taos."

Longarm swore. "How long ago did the stagecoach leave?"

The man looked over at a clock on the wall. "About an hour ago."

"And you're sure that's where they were going?"

"That's where they bought tickets for. Is there some problem?"

"Not that you can help with," Longarm called as he spun around and hurried back out into the street. He ran back to the undertaker's office, where he'd left the blue roan tied to a hitching rail.

The undertaker had already unloaded the bodies, and was now untying their horses. "Leaving town already?"

"That's right. Your mayor and his lover boarded the stage for Taos."

"They've got two funeral parlors over there," the man said, a little sarcastically. "Just thought you'd like to know."

"Thanks," Longarm quipped.

"Hey!"

Longarm had just tightened his cinch and mounted his roan when he saw Jake Fernley stumping as fast as he could down the street to speak to him.

"Where are you going with my horse?" the stable man demanded.

Longarm jammed his boots into the stirrups and lifted his reins. He was in too much of a hurry to make conversation. "I'm headed for Taos."

Jake Fernley studied the blue roan, then looked accusingly at Longarm. "You've run this fine animal down and he needs rest and feed. He's dropped fifty pounds or more since you took him from me. Dammit, Marshal, I trusted that you'd take much better care of my horse!"

"I'm sorry," Longarm said, feeling ashamed of himself. "I . . . I've had to do some hard riding. But I'll—"

The one-legged man was furious. "You'll pay me an extra five dollars and give the horse back to me right now!" Jake Fernley demanded, reaching for the horse's bit.

"Sorry," Longarm yelled as he kicked the roan in the flanks and sent it bolting forward. "But I'll be back by tomorrow to pay you! Next day at the latest!"

"You can't steal my best horse! You're a federal marshal, dammit!"

As he galloped hard out of town, Longarm thought about how he sure would have liked to have had the time to swap the exhausted roan for one of Jake Fernley's fresh mounts. But, on the other hand, he had the feeling that Jake wouldn't let him rent another good horse at *any* price. So he just kept the roan running as he tore out of Montezuma riding north.

With any luck at all, he might be able to overtake the stagecoach before it reached Taos. If he could do that, it would make arresting Ward and the widow woman a whole lot easier.

Chapter 19

Longarm was saddle sore and every bit as worn down as the roan, but he kept pushing the fast pace. The road north between Montezuma and Taos was scenic and well traveled. Huge pines and high, craggy mountains surrounded him on all sides, and Longarm saw several herds of deer as well as a big bull elk that he startled into the heavy growth of trees that lined the road.

The severe storm of the previous day had passed and the weather had turned warm. As Longarm pushed the blue roan as fast as he dared, the played-out animal began to sweat profusely. Fearing the horse would collapse and die if he did not stop, Longarm reluctantly drew rein at a mountain stream and let the animal drink sparingly as it caught its breath.

"We can't be far behind that stagecoach," he told the roan in a note of encouragement. "That last grade we climbed at a trot would have to have been taken at a much slower pace by the stagecoach. I'm sure we're less than two or three miles behind them. Don't give up on me now."

Suddenly, a man and his wife riding a buckboard came bouncing down the road moving south, and Longarm remounted his exhausted horse and intercepted them. "Hello!"

"Hello!" the driver called in greeting.

"How far ahead is the stagecoach bound for Taos?" Longarm asked. "You must have passed it not long ago."

"We did for a fact. It's not more than a mile ahead up the road." The driver of the buckboard looked at the roan with concern. "That roan is pretty heated and used up today, mister. Maybe you should dismount and let him rest a bit longer."

"I wish that I could," Longarm replied, tipping his hat at the man's wife and setting off at a slow gallop.

The roan was game and he was more than tough. Longarm didn't have to whip the animal to make it gallop, and after a short time he finally saw the stagecoach stopped at a stage station. The station consisted of a shack, a few corrals, and a couple of small barns. Longarm supposed this was a place where the passengers could stretch their legs and the team could get some grain and a breather before pressing on the rest of the way into Taos. In this high country with its many ups and downs, horses had to be rested far more frequently than on the flatter and lower elevations.

Longarm rode into some aspen and dismounted. He could see that there were about eight or nine people milling around the station and some of them were children. Longarm did not want to brace Doug Ward in front of children and have to kill the man before their young eyes. And then there was the matter of Mrs. Trotter. She might very well be packing a pistol and more than willing to use it before she'd allow herself to be arrested for multiple murders.

Longarm gave the situation his most careful thought. Once the pair of killers were back inside the stagecoach, it would be hard for him to make an arrest. He decided that he might be able to circle around the station and then come in from behind and catch the mayor and the Trotter woman by surprise.

"Come on!" he urged the roan. "We have to get out behind that station now before they board the stagecoach."

Longarm sent the roan plunging through heavy aspen, pines, and tangled undergrowth. He rode almost blindly as he was being whipped by branches and thickets, and the horse kept having to jump treacherous deadfalls. Finally, Longarm had circled the station. He dismounted and tied the sweaty and gasping roan to an aspen.

He drew his Winchester from the saddle boot and made sure his Colt revolver had not become dislodged and lost during the last few minutes of his wild ride through the trees. Satisfied that his weapons were ready and available, Longarm started working his way forward with every intention of ending up right behind the station. Once having done that, he felt sure he could step out of cover and get the drop on Ward and Mrs. Trotter before the man could shoot or run.

But Longarm hadn't counted on two big station dogs that saw him sneaking through the forest. The dogs began to bark, and they attacked Longarm with teeth bared. Longarm had to club one of them with the stock of his Winchester, and he almost had to shoot the other one before he booted it in the head and sent it howling back toward the stage station.

But worse, *far* worse, was the fact that everyone had stopped what they were doing and were staring at him as if he were crazy.

Linda Trotter, whom Longarm now thought of as a black widow, and Doug Ward stood frozen for a moment, and then both realized with a visible start that it was Marshal Custis Long charging forward to arrest them for murder.

Ward broke from the others and ran to a horse that was saddled nearby. He was carrying a pair of heavily laden saddlebags, but the man was athletic enough to leap on the horse and send it flying up the road toward Taos.

Mrs. Linda Trotter was not nearly so agile, but she was brave, inventive, and resourceful. She reached into a large purse, grabbed a revolver, and shouted, "He's a killer! He's come to kill me! Help!"

Everyone froze in shock as Longarm continued running toward the station. Linda Trotter looked around for some fool to jump in and try to help her kill Longarm, but no one moved to her aid, so she raised the pistol and began firing.

Longarm felt a bullet cut at his earlobe. Another bullet plucked his sleeve, and then he skidded to a halt, raised the Winchester, and took aim.

"Drop it, Mrs. Trotter!"

Instead of surrendering, she kept firing, so he shot the woman right through what would ordinarily have been a heart. But he now understood that the beautiful widow Linda Trotter didn't have a heart, just a hole filled with treachery, cunning, and greed.

Women and children screamed and scattered. Two men looked as if they wanted to go for their guns, until

Longarm yelled, "I'm a United States Marshal! Don't anyone move!"

To make sure they believed him, Longarm dropped the rifle and ripped his badge from his inside coat pocket with one hand while drawing his six-gun with his other hand.

The stagecoach driver and the others threw up their hands as if they had been jabbed in the ass with a red-hot poker. One yelled, "Don't kill us, Marshal! Don't shoot!"

Longarm replaced his badge and hurried over to Linda Trotter. He checked her pulse, found none, and said, "This woman is a cold-blooded murderer. The man she was with was her accomplice. I've got to catch him and my horse is tied back in the trees and he's just worn out. Who's got a horse I can use?"

There was great urgency in his voice, and the stagecoach driver said, "There are a couple of company horses in the corral. The buckskin is the best and fastest one."

Longarm glanced over at the buckskin. Like the blue roan, it was tall and rangy. "Saddle him and do it fast!" he shouted.

The stagecoach driver jumped into a run. He grabbed a rope and then vaulted over the top rail to catch the buckskin. Longarm saw the man rush the horse into one of the barns, and knew that it would be saddled and ready to ride in minutes.

"Marshal, do you realize what a terrible shock you just gave my little children?" a man in a nice suit finally had the nerve to demand. "You shot a *woman* to death in front of their little eyes!"

"I know and I'm really, really sorry," Longarm said, meaning every word of it. "But as you might have noticed, she was shooting at me and it was a matter of kill or be killed."

"You're wounded, Marshal," another man said, yanking a clean handkerchief out of his pocket. "You need bandaging."

"I'm not hurt much. Right now, I need to finish up this bloody business by catching that killer," Longarm countered.

"But he's the mayor of Montezuma!"

"Yeah," Longarm said, "and isn't that one helluva sorry joke."

Before the man could think up a suitable reply, Longarm mounted the buckskin as it was led out of the corral at a trot. With his Winchester in one hand and the reins in the other, he sent the tall buckskin galloping out of the yard after the mayor.

Longarm let the buckskin run, and it flew up the hard-packed dirt road. "Unless Mayor Ward was lucky enough to steal a Thoroughbred back at the station just minutes ago," Longarm said to himself, "I'm gonna catch and kill that murdering sonofabitch!"

After about a mile, Longarm finally caught sight of the fleeing Doug Ward up ahead. The man glanced back over his shoulder and saw Longarm and the buckskin with its ears pinned back and its front legs flying.

"It's over!" Longarm yelled at the top of his lungs.

Ward twisted in his saddle and fired two shots, hoping to hit Longarm or his horse and bring them down. That told Longarm that the murdering mayor had no intention of being taken alive.

Chapter 20

The mayor of Montezuma disappeared in a cloud of dust around a sharp bend in the road just up ahead. Longarm was about a hundred yards behind the killer and bent low in his saddle, urging the animal to run full out. But when he came around the bend, to Longarm's shock and dismay, there was Doug Ward standing half hidden behind a pine waiting in ambush. Longarm felt helpless as he watched the man raise his gun to take dead aim at him or perhaps the tall buckskin, which offered a big, easy target. Longarm realized in an instant that if his buckskin took a well-placed bullet, it would cartwheel and he would be thrown hard and either injured or killed.

Either way, Doug Ward would have him at his mercy.

Longarm yanked sideways on the reins while throwing his full weight to the right. Ward fired and his bullet creased the buckskin's left shoulder, and then sliced through saddle leather just above Longarm's boot top. Thrown violently off stride, the buckskin lost its footing and tumbled down a steep incline into a maze of rocks and heavy underbrush.

Longarm momentarily lost consciousness. A few seconds later, he was dimly aware that the buckskin was on top of him thrashing wildly. Longarm couldn't get his right leg out from under the terrified animal, and he felt a jolt of pain where the lower leg was pinned against the rocky ground.

Suddenly, the buckskin was up and staggering into the forest. The dazed and injured horse took a few unsteady steps, then came to a halt with its head down and chest heaving in a picture of confusion.

Longarm heard the pounding of boots just above him on the road. He turned his attention upward and saw Doug Ward lining up a fatal gunshot. For a moment, their eyes locked, and then Ward fired, missing. Longarm rolled deeper into the underbrush, clawing for his gun and amazed to discover it and his holster had not been torn away.

"You sonofabitch!" Ward screamed, squinting downward into the brush and then firing again.

Longarm was scraped, bruised, bleeding, and his leg was broken. He was half-blinded by grit, but he started shooting up at the blurry figure of Ward just as fast as he could squeeze the trigger.

Ward hadn't expected Longarm to be able to return fire after taking such a spectacular plummet off the road and down into a low gully. It didn't seem possible that any horseman could have survived such a bad accident. But Longarm *had* survived and as he began to fire, Doug Ward started to dance as the heavy impact of bullets stitched his clean white shirtfront. An expression of wild triumph was replaced by a dumbfounded look of profound disbelief just a moment before Ward tumbled down into the gully with his gun still clenched in his lifeless fist.

Longarm's senses were swimming, and it took everything he had left to struggle upright and limp over to Ward's body. He searched the man and found over six thousand dollars that had almost certainly come from the sale of Diablo Peak gold.

Keeping his weight off his broken leg, Longarm turned to his buckskin. The horse was scraped up and bleeding, but it had escaped a fatal bullet thanks to Longarm's desperate act of throwing its weight sideways. Longarm hobbled over to the animal and began stroking its neck and talking in a soft, soothing voice. When the gelding finally grew calm, he managed to lead it over to a rock, where he mounted with great difficulty and rode back up to the road.

The saddlebags that Doug Ward had dropped near a pine tree were stuffed with gold and greenbacks. Gritting his teeth against waves of pain, Longarm tied the saddlebags to his own saddle. Fighting off waves of pain and nausea, he somehow managed to remount and then turn his horse back toward the stage station, worried that he was going to lose consciousness. But he gritted his teeth and felt a huge sense of accomplishment because every last person responsible for the Montezuma murders was now dead.

When he arrived back at the stage station, Longarm asked the station tender to get a knife and slit his boot top because it was becoming painfully tight.

179

"My gawd, Marshal, that leg is broken!"

"Is the bone sticking out?" Longarm asked, hanging on to his saddle horn and trying not to fall.

"No, it ain't," the man said, "but it's still a bad break."

Longarm took a couple of deep breaths and looked down at the stagecoach passengers. "I don't suppose any of you is a doctor?"

The passengers shook their heads.

"Help me down and let's get my leg straightened and splinted before the swelling gets even worse."

They eased him off the buckskin, which was still shaken and trembling.

Longarm said, "Someone take care of this horse. Put some liniment on his shoulder wound and lead him around slow and easy for a while. Sometimes a horse that's been through what this one has can go into shock."

"I don't know how you can stand the pain," a woman said, staring at Longarm's broken leg. "That looks like it must hurt something awful!"

"I've had worse happen to me," Longarm told her.

With the help of more people than were really necessary, Longarm got his boot sliced completely off and his pants leg cut away up to the knee. Then, with two men hanging on to each of his arms and the station tender grabbing his foot, they yanked hard.

One of the women fainted and after that, Longarm didn't remember anything.

Chapter 21

Two weeks later, Longarm lay naked in bed with his leg still splinted and Loretta Wilson bouncing up and down on his stiff rod. Her red lips were drawn back and her hair was swishing from side to side as she moaned with unconcealed pleasure.

"Oh, Custis! I don't want to ever stop! Am I hurting your leg, darling?"

"No," he panted, "you're making me feel good all over. Keep it up!"

"No," she growled, "*you* keep it up!"

A good Santa Fe doctor had placed a medical splint on Longarm's broken lower leg and predicted it would mend just fine. But Longarm wasn't thinking about his leg just now. He was enjoying this extended convalescence and ignoring the telegrams from Billy Vail wishing him a speedy recovery and urging him to return to Denver as soon as possible.

Longarm heard the floor creak just outside Loretta's bedroom door, and he gasped, "Oh, no! It's your folks!"

"Don't worry. They can't hear a thing and my door is locked!"

Loretta wasn't about to stop making love until they were both satisfied. Minutes later, that happened and she screamed with pleasure as Longarm spewed his seed.

"Loretta! Loretta, are you all right in there!"

They both heard knocking on Loretta's door, and saw her doorknob turn slightly. But thank heavens it was locked.

"I'm fine, Mother!"

"Oh, goodness gracious! I thought I heard you cry out."

She shouted, "It must have been our cat, Mother!"

Longarm had to bite the back of his hand to keep from bursting out in laughter. "My gawd," he said. "Your *cat*?"

"I told you they were almost stone deaf, and sometimes they sit in their rocking chairs and roll over our cat's tail on the hardwood floor. When they do, she really lets out a screech."

Longarm was in near hysterics. When he finally got control, he shook his head and eased his splinted leg a little to one side where it was a bit more comfortable. "Loretta, are you sure that Vice President Arthur has canceled his trip out here to Santa Fe?"

She hugged him and kissed his cheek. "Of course I am. I have my sources of information and they've never steered me wrong. They tell me that the vice president's secretary sent a telegram yesterday saying he'd come down with some kind of stomach illness and reluctantly

182

had to postpone his western tour. But you know what I think really happened?"

Longarm knew he was going to hear Loretta tell him what she thought anyway, so he asked, "What?"

"I think that the word got out to the vice president that Diablo Peak's vein of gold petered out completely. The boom suddenly went bust. And since the Diablo gold strike no longer existed, there was no real need for the vice president to visit Santa Fe."

Longarm figured that made perfectly good sense. "Then I guess the land will stay in the public's hands."

"I'm sure that it will," she told him. "And that makes the Zuni very happy. You see, they knew that gold was being illegally mined on their sacred peak. And after what happened in the Black Hills when that gold was discovered . . . well, they could see that they would surely lose their sacred Diablo Peak in a gold rush. Now, nobody wants Diablo Peak except them."

"So everyone is happy."

Her smile faded. "I wish that were true, Custis. But my brother was murdered and some other good people were murdered."

Longarm stared up at the ceiling. "Loretta, I'll probably be able to travel in another week."

"Uh-uh," she said, shaking her head and quickly brightening. "I had a talk with your doctor just this morning, and he said you need to stay right here in this bed and rest for another whole month."

"A month!" Longarm exclaimed.

"Yes," Loretta said, trying to look very serious and concerned. "At least that long."

"It's only one bone."

Her hand slid down to his manhood and quickly stroked it back to full attention. "I know, darling. But we want it to stay big and hard, now don't we?"

Longarm suddenly understood her *real* meaning, and then he threw back his head and couldn't stop laughing.

Watch for

**LONGARM AND THE
MYSTERIOUS MR. JIGGS**

the 355th novel in the exciting LONGARM
series from Jove

Coming in June!

GIANT-SIZED ADVENTURE FROM AVENGING ANGEL LONGARM.

BY TABOR EVANS

2006 Giant Edition:
LONGARM AND THE OUTLAW EMPRESS

2007 Giant Edition:
LONGARM AND THE GOLDEN EAGLE SHOOT-OUT

penguin.com

M229AS1207

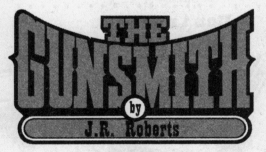

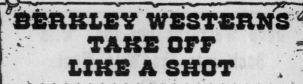